PAST TRANSGRESSIONS

A MASON NASH NOVEL

DAVE SINCLAIR

ALSO BY DAVE SINCLAIR

Mason Nash Novels

Past Transgressions

Shadow Hunting

Devil's End

Atticus Wolfe Novels

Out of Time

It Takes a Spy

The Coldest War

Charles Bishop Novels

Kiss My Assassin

Agent Provocateur

Venetian Blonde

Eva Destruction Novels

The Barista's Guide to Espionage

The Rookie's Guide to Espionage (novella)

The Amnesiac's Guide to Espionage

The Dead Spy's Guide to Espionage

For you, the reader.
Thank you for being on this crazy writer adventure with me.

CHAPTER
ONE

Devil's End was the type of town tourists would call quintessentially English. A Benedictine Abbey overlooked picture-postcard streets lined with stone cottages, surrounded by rolling green countryside. It was a quiet, sleepy Cotswold town. Quiet was exactly what the newest resident of Devil's End sought.

Late-afternoon grey clouds hung low over the cobblestoned streets, somewhat tarnishing the picturesque scene. Stuffing his hands deep in his pockets to ward off the incoming chill, Mason Nash walked briskly.

Facing the small town square, the Hangman's Inn was a Tudor building that had been heavily renovated over the centuries, but still somehow retained its quaint charm. It was hard to know if any part of the four-hundred-year-old pub was original. Not that Nash cared as he opened the front door and was enveloped by the warmth of the pub's open fireplace.

As he strode in, a few of the locals bobbed their head in Nash's direction. Denise, the publican, gave him a friendly wave. It had taken six months to even achieve this landmark level of acknowledgement. Devil's End was a place where ten-year residents were still referred to as newcomers.

Taking up his usual position at a table at the rear of the pub, Nash took off his coat, pulled out his book and gave a shiver to shed the last of the outside cold. Settling in for the evening, he began to read.

The small smattering of locals populated tables and booths in the low-ceilinged pub. The bar took up one entire wall. Deep chocolate wood, it was decorated with exotic bottles and knick-knacks accumulated over the pub's long history. High above the bar, a weathered wooden plaque reminded patrons they were in the Hangman's Inn. If that wasn't subtle enough, on one side was a noose, on the other a real-looking shotgun.

"Alright, love?"

Nash looked up to see a pretty young waitress beaming down at him. Since he'd turned fifty he deemed everyone under thirty-five as young. With a shock of grey hair and matching beard, Nash would never be mistaken for a young man, despite his strict weights and fitness regime.

"Pint of Newcastle Brown and today's special, cheers."

The pub's kitchen had had the same daily special for the last six months. Nash didn't mind. The shepherd's pie was hearty and exactly what he needed to fend off the chill of the evening.

Making a note in her pad, the waitress didn't immediately leave. Instead, she leaned towards the book in his hands. "Bit of light reading?"

Turning over the heavy tome, Nash chuckled. "Just learning about some local history. I'm up to the witch trials around these parts. I didn't know the town had such a colourful past."

"You don't name a town Devil's End after a nice tree." The waitress laughed before her face turned solemn. "This place has a dark past, more than most."

Nash smiled. "I can relate."

Seemingly in no hurry, the waitress asked, "You're the new history teacher up at the high school?"

"And I'm not even wearing a jacket with elbow patches." He held out his hand. "Edmond Green."

It was a name Nash was still getting used to.

Taking his calloused hand in her soft one, she replied, "Lila, Lila Pickford."

"Nice to formally meet you, Lila. How did you know who I was?"

"Small town." She shrugged. "Everyone knows everyone." Lila flicked a finger in his direction. "I've seen you, up on Pertwee hill, just sitting there for hours on end. I've always wondered, what are you doing up there?"

"Meditating. I picked it up when I was bumming around India."

"Like, as in thinking about nothing?"

"Ultimately, I guess. It's more a tranquil mind exercise. It's about noticing your thoughts but offering no judgement on them. Getting into a deep state of relaxation and reducing the noise of the world."

"Oh, right. That's cool." Lila appeared genuinely interested, or at least was managing a close approximation of it. "I imagine the life of a teacher must be pretty stressful."

It took an effort for Nash not to laugh out loud. "They're not the bad thoughts I'm blocking."

Nash imagined he'd give the poor woman nightmares if he ever shared the memories he so desperately tried to suppress. His past life was not one he wanted to relive. Meditation helped make it seem like another time, long

3

ago, but ultimately he had to learn to live with the man he'd once been. The *new* Nash really tried to embody the practice of Ahimsa, the ancient Indian principle of nonviolence, which states that all acts of violence have karmic consequences.

In keeping with those principles he would have preferred a more ethical, less meat-oriented option for his dinner, but the pub offered no vegetarian options, so the shepherd's pie would have to do. He was making a concerted effort to get to know the townsfolk and the pub was the perfect place to present himself as just another resident of the sleepy Devil's End.

If he were twenty years younger Nash wouldn't have minded getting to know Lila better. Quick to smile, great skin, dimples and mischievous eyes; she was just his type. Unfortunately, his years of picking up bar staff had long passed. Even though he was still fit, there was more grey hair than brown, he had to hope his salt-and-pepper beard made him look distinguished rather than old. He'd let Lila be a distracting little daydream and leave it as that.

But there was something about her he couldn't immediately dismiss. She reminded Nash of someone, but for the life of him he couldn't remember who. Then again, at his age everyone reminded him of someone. This memory was different, though; important and certainly buried. So many buried memories. It's what happened when you spent half your life performing tasks that would give civilians a lifetime of nightmares. Nash did his best to bury his past deep, but some memories would randomly jump out without warning. Sometimes for days at a time. Those were not good days.

"Hey there, you're a million miles away." Lila waved her

notepad before his eyes. "You having an out-of-body experience there?"

"I've only had one of those and that was at a Red Hot Chilli Peppers concert."

Smirking, Lika asked, "The who?"

"No, they were before my time."

Laughing out loud, she replied, "You're funny."

"I have my moments."

In no apparent hurry to get back to work, she asked, "You always take the same seat, why is that?"

The question gave Nash pause. He tilted his head. "I don't think I do..."

"Yeah, every time. Up the back, facing the door." She turned towards the thinly populated establishment. "You can see the whole pub from here."

The fighting seat, Nash's old SAS instructor had called it. It had been ingrained in him for so long he'd forgotten he still did it. Select the most easily defendable position in any situation. Old habits die hard.

He found it amusing that despite his chosen path of pacifism he was still practising the habits established in his more brutal past. The old ways weren't exactly in keeping with the philosophy of the non-violent yama of Ahimsa. Perhaps the new Nash wasn't as enlightened as he'd thought.

"Seems I'll have to change things up if I'm getting predictable."

"Nothing wrong with predictable." Lila curled the ends of her long dirty blonde hair coquettishly. "There's many a local lady in these parts who'd like a predictable, eligible man such as yourself."

"Many?" Nash shifted uncomfortably in his seat. This was turning into a less staid evening than he'd envisaged.

"Oh, for sure." Lila tucked a stray hair behind her ear. "You're quite the topic of discussion in the local spinsters' network."

"I am?"

"A good-looking man who reads more than the football results, doesn't smell of manure and has all his teeth? Darlin', you're a catch." She laughed, but there was determination in her eyes. "And I should know."

"And how would the local spinsters' network know I'm eligible?"

She leaned forward—very forward. Her lips lightly brushed his ear as she whispered throatily, "Small town." Taking her time to rise to her full height, Lila seemed to enjoy the surprised expression on his face.

Giving him a wink, she said, "I'll put your order in and get you that pint." She spun and gave him a kittenish grin which brought out her dimples. "You just let me know if there's any way I can service you."

As she disappeared behind the bar Nash blinked several times. He wasn't entirely sure what had just happened. He did his best to focus on his book, but the words floated around the page, stubbornly refusing to coalesce into anything legible.

Abandoning the effort, Nash looked up and took in the pub. There were a few regular faces who seemingly never left the confines of the Hangman's Inn. As he looked around, he saw a couple enter and immediately gravitate towards the far booth. Dressed in black, they picked the darkest part of the tavern. They were dressed far better than the locals—even at this distance, Nash could tell they wore designer outfits. Their haircuts were expensive, as was their sturdy footwear. But that wasn't what drew Nash's attention.

The man and the woman were doing their best to appear casual, but their taut muscles betrayed their supposed outward calm. It was their frequent faux-casual glances around the pub that gave away their intent. It seemed their focus was directed at one thing in particular: Nash.

After all these years, picking the fighting seat still had its advantages.

About to dismiss his observations as an overly vigilant relic of a past life, Nash noticed a man pacing outside. Through the front tavern window, he watched the man, dressed similarly to the couple and with an equally expensive haircut, walking up and back in front of the pub. One could call it patrolling. If the man's earpiece wasn't enough to dispel Nash's concerns that he was being overly cautious, the handgun-shaped bulge under the man jacket certainly was. The man walked away from the pub, square-jawed and determined. *Where are you going, man?*

"Newcastle."

Nash stood and walked to the bar where the publican Denise held his pint aloft. He took it with a bob of his head. His pacifist leanings contorted within the depths of his subconscious.

Keeping his voice low, he whispered, "Hey Denise, there's something I've been meaning to ask. That shotgun over the bar, it wouldn't happen to be real, would it?"

"That, love?" She chortled. "In this country? God, no. Barrel was welded shut years ago, why'd you ask?"

"No reason." Nash did his best to keep his gaze off the newly arrived couple. "You mind if I grab my cutlery now?"

"Lila will bring it over, but feel free to grab some if you want, love."

Nash gave her the thumbs-up and proceeded to the

wooden cutlery trays, napkins and condiments at the end of the bar. Picking up a salt and pepper shaker, he used a large paper napkin to conceal the fistful of heavy wooden-handled steak knives. Returning to his table, he placed his stash beside him, away from prying eyes. Under the pretence of reading his book, Nash used the reflective surfaces around the bar to keep an eye on his new friends.

The likeliest explanation was that he was being overly paranoid and the well-dressed couple were nothing more than that. The yogi in him wished it was true. It was entirely possible the man out the front wore a hearing aid, and the bulge in his pocket was nothing more sinister than a pair of sunglasses. But Nash's years of training and experience told him these simple explanations were wrong. He couldn't pinpoint the precise reason he was on edge, but every fibre of his being told him these people were here to do him harm.

As much as the *new* Nash tried to adhere to Gandhi's principles of non-violence, the old Mason Nash wasn't about to make it easy for them.

Visualising potential assault scenarios, Nash mentally walked through various counterattack strategies. Flexing and unflexing his hands, he did his best to prepare for the inevitable fight.

From the corner of his eye, he saw the woman issue a subtle nod as the man stood. A non-verbal sign of approval.

Oh, come on guys, that's sloppy.

Noticing the man stalking towards him, Nash raised his head from his supposed reading and faced the man front-on for the first time. There was no doubt in Nash's mind now. The man reached into his jacket.

As his fingers encircled the hilt of the steak knife, Nash resumed the persona of the man he'd vowed to never be again. Self-preservation trumped philosophy, it seemed. The swinging doors of the kitchen flung open and Lila emerged with a big plate and an even bigger smile. Nash's eyes narrowed on the man in the centre of the room as he followed Lila's progress. He was going to use her approach as cover.

Swinging her hips, Lila beamed at Nash. "I asked chef to put extra cheese on top. Trust me, it takes it to a whole new level. Well, as much as Mich's cooking can."

Nash stood. The unexpected move had an immediate effect. Lila's cheery demeanour was muted by the sudden and aggressive move. And the man in the centre of the room reeled as he extracted a Glock G20.

The sight of the gun didn't panic Nash like it would most history teachers. He'd seen plenty in his time. "Whatever this is, you don't have to do it. We can find a peaceful way out of this."

The man tilted his head ever so slightly, as if surprised by the reaction from Nash. The moment of curiosity remained precisely that: a moment. Nash watched the muscles in the man's neck twitch and the slightest of tightening of his grip on the pistol. There was only one way this was going to end.

Oh hell.

As the man stepped forward, determination etched across his face, Nash yelled, "Lila, down!"

The waitress was too shocked to heed Nash's order, so he grasped her shoulder and forcibly pushed her aside, sending his food crashing to the floor. A deafening gunshot rang out, but it was rushed and went wide. Nash ducked low with a knife in each hand and sprinted to the left, forcing the assassin to adjust his aim. That moment was all

Nash needed. He darted to the right and threw the steak knife at the man's exposed chest.

Before the assassin could unleash another shot, the knife found its mark in the man's shoulder. He screamed as his shot embedded itself into the ceiling. The knife blade wasn't lodged deep, and thankfully the wound didn't appear to be fatal, but Nash was impressed that the piece of cutlery had even managed to do that much.

The two patrons closest to the door made the sensible choice and scrambled out of the pub. The assassin's companion held back, apparently waiting to see how things would play out. Nash was both personally thankful and—as a professional—disgusted with her choice. You always backed your partner. In a fight for your life, "fair" didn't enter into it.

The woman pressed her ear and practically yelled, "Under attack by target. Get back here, *now!*"

Nash figured she was calling back the third member of the group. If it were Nash, he'd have positioned a third shooter at his home in case the first two failed. The woman wasn't holding off her attack because she wanted a fair fight, she was waiting for backup.

Crying in pain, the first assassin slapped the wooden-handled knife from his shoulder and lifted his weapon once more, though his hand was far more unsteady now.

Rushing towards his foe, Nash breathed out, "Sorry, Gandhi."

The knife must have hit an axillary artery, as a deep red seeped above his jacket. Before the assassin could take aim, Nash acted on instinct and thrust the man's arm upward, sending a round booming through the confines of the pub. With the man's arm aloft, Nash plunged the other steak knife deep into the man's firing arm, between the radius and the ulna. He twisted it for good measure, then tugged downward to open the wound even wider.

Filipino martial arts had taught Nash that the opponent's hand should be his top priority. De-fanging the snake, his intense instructor had called it, and that had been Nash's intent. However, despite the horrendous injury, the assassin still held the Glock in his trembling hand and was gritting his teeth as he bent the barrel towards Nash.

Groaning as he held the muscular arm at bay, Nash said, "Don't, please." He watched the gun barrel tilt towards him. "I don't want to..."

Another shot rang in his ears. It was immediately followed by a scream. Nash's gaze darted to see Lila cowering under his table with her hands over her head, shaking in fear. A large chunk of the corner of the table above her head was missing.

The assassin noted Nash's reaction and aimed the pistol in Lila's direction.

"Stop this, please." Nash heard the desperation in his own voice.

Between clenched teeth, the assassin groaned, "Fuck you."

The man wouldn't stop. Nash had no choice. *Fuck you for making me do this.*

Extracting the knife from the assassin's arm, Nash repeatedly stabbed the man's side, sending geysers of blood spurting from the wounds. It was a savage blow but, assuming he sought immediate hospital care, a non-fatal one. Weakened, legs buckling, the big man cried in agony.

The assassin's pistol clattered to the floor. Nash held the now-crumbling body upright, scanning for the man's companion. It didn't take long to find her. She advanced towards him, hand in her jacket, wrath in her eyes. She wasn't firing; she must have known her partner was still alive. To challenge that notion, Nash pushed the heavy body towards her. As she reeled backwards, Nash flung the knife at her, but it was so slick with blood it didn't release correctly and instead sailed harmlessly overhead, clanging against the bottles behind the bar.

The moaning man's gun had fallen near the front entrance, too far away for Nash to reach it before the woman could get off her first shot. Instead, he launched himself at her, slapping the gun from her hand as she raised it. It flew through the air, landing heavily on the big bar near the cutlery trays.

Their gazes followed the clanging pistol and as one, they raced for the weapon. Nash was slightly to the left and he arrived a fraction of a second behind. As his opponent reached for the Glock, Nash brought down a newly acquired steak knife through the back of her hand, halting its advance an inch short of its target.

Screaming in agony, the woman doubled down her cries of pain as Nash bashed the hilt of the blade deeper into the wood of the bar. Grasping her other wrist, Nash contorted his body to grab another steak knife. He slammed her undamaged hand on the bar and drove the knife through the other palm.

The woman's screams intermingled with the cries of her companion slumped on the floor. Both individuals had chosen violence this day, and Nash had been forced to meet that choice with an equivalent response, but he wanted no more. He could easily have taken both their lives, but that was something Nash had vowed never to do again, and he wasn't about to break his oath if he could avoid it. He'd incapacitated the assailants, but kept them alive for medical assistance and, almost importantly, questioning. He had many questions.

Picking up the pistol, Nash heard the front door swing open. Without turning, he dove to the ground and rolled as the sound of machine-gun fire erupted in the confined space. Darting behind a table, Nash flipped it to offer some semblance of cover as bullets strafed the tavern.

From his cover, Nash yelled, "You people are really messing with my Ahimsa here!"

He cast an eye around the room to see the terrified civilians under fire. The madman who had entered didn't care where his bullets struck. They'd all be dead within seconds unless he was stopped.

Nash let out a defeated sigh and gripped the pistol tight. Waiting for his moment, he feinted left before darting the right and emerging from behind the table. He fired a single bullet into the remaining assassin's forehead.

All gunfire ceased as the man collapsed backward. Nash dropped his gun to the floor, feeling nauseous to his core. Turning to the bar, his shoulders slumped.

"Why did you make me..." He scratched the back of his neck. "I didn't want to..."

The assassin on the floor was now silent, a bullet in his skull courtesy of his comrade's erratic gunfire. The assassin Nash had pinned to the bar was now streaked with bullet holes, her body slumped, dangling in a grotesque impromptu crucifixion.

Inhaling unsteadily, Nash drew on the practice he'd learned in India to slow his inhalations in the futile hope he could calm his thoughts. Forcing himself into the moment, he assessed the damage. He found it ironic he was using his eastern training at a time like this. First and foremost, the locals appeared unhurt. Only the three assassins bore fatal wounds, everyone else was unharmed, at least physically. The tavern was shot up but easily repaired; the locals' nerves, not so much.

The pub's patrons unsteadily began to emerge from their impromptu hiding spots. Nash leaned down and offered his hand to Lila, who stared at it, uncomprehending. Shock. They would all need blankets and warm drinks. But that would have to wait.

Standing, he addressed the room. "Everything is okay now." Nash realised his voice was as steady as his hands. "You're safe. It's over." He turned towards the permed blonde head emerging from behind the bar. "Hi, Denise." He plastered on the friendliest tone he could manage. "Uh, would you mind calling the police?"

Face white as bleached sheets, Denise stuttered, "Who were they?"

"That," he exhaled, feeling more aches than he had in years, "is something I intend to find out."

CHAPTER
TWO

"Cutlery?"

"That's what I said." Nash had been over the story so many times he had no emotion left to invest in his timbre. "Namely steak knives." He sighed. "As I told," he pointed to the contingent of police and emergency services workers huddled together in the dark town square, "him, him, her, her and him."

Nash sat on the kerb outside the Hangman's Inn, a silver thermal blanket draped around his shoulders. Before him stood a squat superintendent, with a notepad and a distinctly sceptical demeanour.

The police officer pushed his peaked cap back with his pencil. "Well, I'm the one asking the questions now, sir."

"Obviously. I can tell by the copious stream of verbal effluent cascading from you." Nash rubbed his hands down his face. "How many fucking times do I have to tell the same *fucking* story?"

The superintendent's pencil snapped as his eyes cast daggers at Nash.

"I think we could all do with a bit of a break."

Nash turned from the superintendent's pasty, reddening face to the newcomer who seemed to have appeared out of nowhere. Nash smiled. It was the first genuine moment of joy he'd had in the hours since this whole mess began.

The newcomer flashed his ID card and led the still-riled police officer a few paces away to have a quiet word. It took only a few moments before the superintendent capitulated and wandered off to the clutch of police pouring tea under a temporary tent set up in the square.

The new man sat down on the kerb next to Nash with a grunt. He was tall, and had further to travel.

Nash shook the newcomer's hand. "Was I snippy?"

In reply, Nash's new companion slowly shook his head. "I think the use of the phrase verbal effluent indicated the train had well and truly departed Reasonable Station and was thoroughly on its way to Snippy Town."

"I've had a bit of a day." Nash leaned over and shouted towards the departing superintendent, "Sorry, I've had a bit of a day!"

In return, the red-faced superintendent gave a half wave and grunted.

Paul Cavendish chuckled. The head of Spec Ops at MI6 had once been Nash's boss, and was one of the few people from those days Nash still genuinely called a friend, though it had been years since they'd last spoken. Tall, gangly and caring, Paul was one of the authentic good guys in an industry of bastards. The often morally ambiguous duties of those in espionage meant "nice" was as rare as platinum, and just as valuable.

Paul also had one the sharpest minds Nash had ever known, not that his lanky facade gave much of an indication. It was a misapprehension Paul had taken advantage of often. People underestimated Paul Cavendish at their peril.

Their friendship had been forged in bullets and blood. They'd bonded over bad fathers and good whiskey. Back in the day they'd traded stories of whose father had inflicted the longest-lasting mental scars. They never had come up with a clear victor. But father's didn't seem on Paul's mind tonight.

Rubbing his hands together for warmth, Paul said, "You've caused quite the ruckus."

Looking at the volume of emergency services vehicles and flashing lights illuminating the sleepy town, Nash replied, "Seems that way."

"An ex-member of MI6 killing three assassins will do that."

"One."

"What's that?"

"I only killed one, and that was an absolute last resort."

"Ah." Paul reached into his pocket and handed Nash a hip flask. "They've thrown everyone at this one. The local cops, heads of the LPA, Border Force, GDSC, MI5, the amalgamated traffic wardens union and the local chapter of the Postman Pat Fan Club. Everyone."

As much as he didn't want to, Nash smiled. "Not all of those are real, are they?"

"No." Paul laughed quietly. "MI5 wouldn't get out of bed for anything less than a terrorist bombing." He grinned. "Good to see you, old friend."

"Go easy on the old." Nash took a sip from Paul's flask and was pleasantly surprised by the expensive tasting whiskey. The man always knew good booze.

Paul laughed. "I thought you and I were done."

"So did I."

It was rare for a senior member of MI6 to attend a domestic disturbance. The organisation had no jurisdiction to operate within the borders of the United Kingdom. Nash wasn't sure if Paul was present due to the senior role he held within MI6, the fact that a past operative had been attacked by professional assassins or because it was Nash in particular. He knew if he asked Paul directly he wouldn't get a straight answer. They were friends, but that didn't mean Paul wasn't executing his own agenda. Instead, the two men passed the hip flask between them and enjoyed a rare moment of quiet.

Emerging from the police-taped front entrance of the Hangman's Inn, a distraught woman stalked hesitantly forward. Like Nash, Lila was covered in a thermal blanket and was bookmarked by two female police officers.

As she passed, Nash asked, "Are you okay, Lila?"

Glaring at him with a mixture of fear and contempt, Lila strode forward mutely. Her legs seemed to move by instinct alone. She ducked into a waiting police car, no doubt there to take the distraught woman home. The vehicle took off without her looking back.

Paul caught the exchange. "Friend of yours?"

Nash sighed. "Seems that's not to be."

Paul watched him curiously but said nothing. A young constable walked past and Nash waved her down. Distracted, her gaze searched the crowd of emergency workers, indicating she had somewhere else to be.

"Excuse me, is the publican about?"

"I'm not sure, sir. Why's that?"

"I didn't pay for my drink." He thought for a moment. "Or dinner, for that matter."

Both the constable and Paul stared at Nash. Paul appeared more amused than the police officer.

"What's that, sir?"

"At the pub, before, ah, the ruckus, I had a pint. I also ordered dinner, which ended up on the floor, but I guess it was my fault it happened. I didn't pay for any of it."

Scowling, the constable waved at the police tape-adorned pub. "I think they have other things to worry about." She pivoted and darted away.

When she was out of earshot Paul chuckled. "I always said you had too many morals for MI6."

"They did get in the way sometimes."

Taking a swig from his flask, Paul didn't turn to Nash as he asked, "Ed Green?"

"What's wrong with Ed Green?"

"It's a bit boring, isn't it?"

Nash leaned back. "That was exactly the point. Being unmemorable to the point of a coma."

Accepting the reply, Paul sat quietly for some time. Nash waited, knowing it was a precisely calculated moment before Paul asked what he really wanted to know. When it came to his job, Paul rarely did anything on a whim.

A beat later, it came: "Any idea who sent assassins after you?"

It took every ounce of Nash's willpower to keep from laughing. It was surprisingly comforting to know that Paul hadn't changed. Nash slowly shook his head.

Inhaling, Paul asked, "Can you think of anyone who would want to kill you?"

They both waited a moment before they broke into laughter. With Nash's history, he'd have accumulated enemies enough to last multiple lifetimes.

In fact, that was one of the reasons Nash had left MI6, though it was nowhere near the top of the list. Mainly, he'd realised he was changing. He no longer wanted to be part of a world of violence. The scene before him only served as an all-too-real reminder.

But there were other reasons he'd quit, too. He'd realised his reactions were getting slower. And then there was the reason he'd chosen not to give during the exit interview: MI6 wasn't the same organisation he'd joined. The bureaucrats ran it now. Bloated and slow, MI6 no longer fought the good fight. The only thing it seemed to be fighting for these days was relevance in a world that had moved on from human spies. MI6 just hadn't realised it yet.

Paul sniffed the night air. "I thought you turned your back on violence."

Nash was too tired to smile. "I did."

Paul watched the last dead body being loaded into the back of a hearse. He tilted his head towards the scene. "There are some who may beg to differ."

Feeling sick to his very core, Nash shook his head slowly. "I vowed when I left the service I'd never take another life. I broke that vow today, Paul. It's unravelled everything I've worked towards in the last few years."

"The way I hear it," Paul nodded to the knot of police in the square, "you saved lives tonight. The only ones who died were those who'd been sent to murder. I can't say I'd lose sleep over that."

"I will." Nash realised how cold his voice sounded. "I'm not the man I used to be."

Paul didn't rush his answer, likely sensing the deep regret Nash felt. "You took one life, not all three, and that was an absolute last resort. This isn't on you, my friend. You did everything you could to ensure no one died. You didn't start this. They did. A manifestation of the old adage of fuck around and find out."

Tilting his head to concede the point, Nash asked, "What can you tell me?"

"Nothing." Paul's voice carried no malice, nor was there the friendly tone he'd used earlier. "You're out of the game now, remember?"

"Tell them that." Nash flicked his thumb towards the body as they closed the rear of the hearse. "They did their best to kill me, Paul. This wasn't some random spur of the moment act. They targeted me, and I have no idea why. You have to give me something."

Paul seemed to be weighing up the request against his oath of professional duty. His sigh told Nash which way the decision fell.

"Nothing you wouldn't expect from professionals. No IDs. No clothing labels. Nothing in their pockets to indicate where they're from. No cigarettes, no gum, absolutely nothing to denote a nationality. They're as clean as if they'd been dipped in acid."

"Prints?"

"They're running them now, but we both know what that will show up."

Nash nodded. "Any car?"

"They haven't found one yet."

Rotating his shoulder, Nash wondered how many injuries he'd sustained fighting the assassins. He felt every one of his years. Mind ticking over, he realised there was one more question he needed to ask.

"Did you send them?"

Instead of being offended by the question, Paul took his time answering—in part, Nash suspected, to show it wasn't a reflex response. "Let's just put it this way: if I had, you wouldn't be alive to buy me a round as soon as that pub opens up again." He patted Nash on the shoulder and he did his best not to wince. "Whoever this team was, they must have been highly paid to try such a brash operation."

Nash finished off the flask. He recalled some of the team's tactics and how at the time he thought the execution was sloppy. Although with his current aches he wasn't as convinced.

"Broad daylight? Civilians around? Why so public? Why not wait until you've had a warm milk and fallen asleep? Far less collateral damage."

"Which tells me two things." Nash watched the hearse drive solemnly away. "One, they don't care about civilians getting in the way."

Paul raised an eyebrow. "And the second?"

"They were on a deadline."

"A deadline for what?"

Nash handed Paul the empty flask and gazed into the night sky. He took in the quietness of the scene. *That's what I intend to find out.*

Nash entered his quaint cottage cautiously. The police had already given it a sweep, but that didn't mean he wasn't on guard. He was thankful he'd managed put his washing away earlier in the day. He didn't want the police finding his unmentionables lying around; it would have been unbecoming.

Taking his time to search every nook and cranny, Nash only relaxed after a thorough search. He hadn't survived this long by being careless.

The cottage was a little splashier than what a regular high school teacher could afford, but not enough to make it obvious. Modern appliances, fresh paintwork and stylish furnishings that complemented the old-school charm of the place. His intent had always been to blend in with the locals—a pipe dream that had been shot to hell the instant assassins had landed in town.

Making his way to the ensuite, he shut the heavy door behind him. The workmen he'd hired to do the renovation thought he was crazy installing a reinforced steel door between the bedroom and attached bathroom. He'd ignored their jibes; they didn't know who he'd crossed in his previous life.

Nash reflected on the reason he'd created the panic room in the first place. Perhaps he wasn't as committed to leaving his old ways behind as he'd thought. Gandhi never had a stash like this.

Pressing the hidden button at the base of his vanity unit, a *click* sounded as a floor tile popped up. Lifting it out of place, Nash regarded the alcove he'd had built into the floor. It was something he'd hoped he'd never use. It was amazing how wrong one man could be. But he wasn't about to head out into the night unprepared.

Extracting two Heckler & Koch USP semiautomatics and two spare magazines, he was surprised at how familiar the deadly weapons felt in his now-civilian hands. Closing his secret hatch, Nash went into his den and retrieved a couple of devices from his previous career. Okay, so he hadn't handed in *all* his equipment when he'd retired from the service. There had been a few select items which the quartermaster had attempted to follow up on with several emails. Nash had responded with vague and unhelpful replies, and she'd eventually given up.

Stashing them in a small backpack along with the spare mags, Nash headed out. It was now past two am and the streets of the sleepy little town were exactly that. Even after the events of the evening, which would be spoken about for years, Devil's End had put itself to bed and slept the sleep of the just. The kind of sleep Nash was incapable of.

Paul had promised to let him know if the case was ever solved, but Nash had little faith that would eventuate. This wasn't a reflection on Paul, more on the lack of priority his former organisation would place on the event. Nash, on the other hand, had taken the encounter exceptionally person-ally. An assassination attempt will do that to a man. He decided to take matters into his own hands—literally.

The hit squad had been well-trained and well-funded. Whoever sent them wasn't doing things by halves. This wasn't a spur of the moment assassination attempt; it had been planned. Now all Nash had to do was find out who'd done the planning.

Walking the streets, Nash realised there was a spring in his step. He had never felt *old* old. Old people felt old. He certainly wasn't old. Sometimes his school friends would pop up on social media and his first reaction would be to think, "they got old", but that didn't apply to Nash. Sure, the slight paunch around his mid-section seemed to be a permanent resident rather than a temporary lodger. Sure, there were more grey hairs on his chest (and elsewhere) than he'd care to acknowledge. And sure, he didn't follow conversations in a crowded room as well as he pretended to, but fifty-five wasn't old.

Old people were old. His parents' generation was old. The ones who talked about seeing the Beatles in concert, or claimed to have been at Woodstock. He was young. Or young-ish. He'd seen the Stone Roses in concert, though he didn't want to think how many years ago that actually was. To Nash, 1996 was, what, ten, fifteen years ago?

He still felt like he did when he was twenty-five. Okay,

perhaps that was a stretch. Maybe thirty-five. He definitely didn't feel fifty-five. If age was a state of mind, then Nash was still in his thirties. Early thirties at that. He just wished someone would tell his back.

He wondered how many years had been shaved off in the last few hours. Nash realised he felt younger than he had in years. It was like he'd grown accustomed to a limb that had atrophied and now it had suddenly become operative once more. He'd done a good job of convincing himself he was happy out of the game, that his new life was replenishing and fulfilling. But with the weight of the Heckler & Kochs and the surge of adrenaline, he knew it was all a lie. He felt like a panther finally let out of its cage, on the hunt once more.

Mason Nash had been living a lie, and it wasn't his newly assumed name. It had taken three assassins to make him realise it. He wondered what else he didn't know.

It took an hour of walking back streets to find what he sought. Brand new and pristine, the black Land Rover Discovery Sport stood out among the battered local vehicles. Tucked in a laneway, it was nowhere near a house and too far away from the town centre to be anything other than deliberately parked out of the way.

Extracting a black device around the size of a small modem, Nash pressed a few buttons and the little gadget did its thing. Modern car keyless remote systems consisted of a key fob transmitter and a receiver inside the vehicle. They most commonly use a frequency of 433.92 MHz in Europe. The gadget was executing a brute force attack—using a spectrum analyser to cycle through all frequencies until it hit the right one.

It took ten minutes before there was a ping on Nash's device and the doors unlocked. He checked the boot. There were two unlocked hard cases. Both were empty, although the foam inserts were the exact dimensions of Glock G20s, the same weapon he'd seen up close only hours before. He slammed the boot shut.

Nestling into the plush leather driver's seat, Nash pulled his rugged laptop from his backpack. Not his day-to-day computer, this one had a very specific function. He plugged it into a USB port under the dash and activated a diagnostic program. It was what mechanics used for servicing and troubleshooting engines, though Nash had a different intent.

Once the program did its thing, he pulled up the trip computer file. It conveniently listed all recent trips, complete with kilometres travelled and time stamps. There were several trips of roughly the same distance. He assumed the team had been holed up locally with a base of operation. Nash typed the distance into the map app on his phone and triangulated possible locations. Unless the assassins set out from the middle of a lake, there was only one possible location. Nash had found the safe house.

Hitting the start button, the engine roared to life. Nash plugged the location into his phone's GPS and put the car into gear.

It only took a few minutes to arrive. The house was hidden from the main road behind rows of trees, but was close enough to three highways. A solid strategic location.

Killing the engine two hundred metres down the road, Nash slipped the spare magazines into his pockets and tucked one of the semiautomatics in the back of his jeans. Grasping the other, he racked the slide and turned off the safety. He'd nearly been killed once tonight, he wasn't about to let them complete the job.

Approaching slowly, Nash slunk low in the shadows of

the tree line. Reaching the last tree, he observed the house for a good five minutes, biding his time. There were no lights, no sign of movement. Not that he trusted either.

Nash moved swiftly. As natural as this state felt, he had to remind himself he was no longer a lethal killing machine. The gun felt heavy in his hands. He finally made his move.

He covered the knee-high grass quickly, gun at the ready, breathing regulated and senses on full alert. He was amazed how natural it felt rushing into danger, long after he'd thought he was done. Instead of trepidation, he was overcome with a rush of the exhilaration he'd missed more than he'd thought possible. It felt truer to his nature than teaching a class ever did.

Reaching the back door, he cracked the lock in seconds and entered silently. Alert for any signs of life, he went from room to room. His first run through found no one, but he made another sweep to be sure. Nothing.

The third run through was more relaxed. Knowing he wouldn't be confronted by anyone who meant him permanent harm, he was able to take more in. There were three bedrooms, each with a small suitcase indicating a short stay. Two men, one woman. The belongings were generic, picked up from any high-street shop. They were packed and ready to bug out following the completion of the job.

The kitchen held meagre supplies, enough for around three days. On the bench, three toothbrushes were sitting in a glass of bleach, no doubt to destroy any trace of DNA. Nash was sure if he dusted for prints he'd find the place wiped clean. Again, he was reminded of the group's competence. Pity they weren't good enough to complete their assignment.

It struck Nash as odd that none of the assassins had a

mobile phone on their person, in the car or in the safe house. Surely there would be some way to communicate to their handlers? Perplexed, he conducted yet another sweep of the house, this time searching for any nook or cranny to hide such a device. Eventually, he found a laptop tucked under a piece of wood on top of a bookshelf.

Given the professionalism already displayed, he doubted opening it would grant him access. He couldn't be that fortunate. Luckily, he had resources who could help him crack the secrets within. At least, he hoped she could.

Tucking his prize under his arm, Nash headed for the front door. That was when he heard it.

The sound was distant, but grew steadily louder. The rhythmic *thrum* stood out against the dead quiet country-side: the unmistakable thudding of a helicopter's rotor blades.

Nash took a moment to run through the situation in his mind. He checked the front door in detail. Then he found it. A thumbnail-sized black device in the doorjamb, virtually undetectable. A tiny red LED flashing.

Nash closed his eyes in frustration. *Amateur move, Nash. Amateur.*

Running to the car, he lost precious moments using his spectrum analyser to reuse his hacked fob frequency. He shoved the laptop in the glove box and started the Range Rover, flooring it as the helicopter roared over a nearby hill and dipped its nose straight at him.

Tearing around the narrow unlit country roads at ludi-crous speeds, Nash kept the sky-borne menace in his rear-view mirror. The Bell AH-1 Cobra was no domestic heli-copter. It was a war machine through and through. Nash estimated it must have been a repurposed ex-military chopper. He didn't have much time to contemplate the chopper's origins, though; he was too busy trying to keep from veering off the dark rural roadways.

Bullets strafed the road beside him and Nash yanked hard on the wheel. Almost hurtling off-road, he managed to keep the Land Rover on the hard shoulder. Dropping the automatic transmission into a lower gear, the engine screamed in protest. Another stream of bullets peppered the vehicle, shattering the rear window. The Cobra pulled up hard to avoid the roadside trees and was forced to cut off the attack, albeit momentarily.

Nash doused the car's lights and wound down the windows to get a bearing on his enemy. He wasn't about to make it easy for them. His night vision was still pretty good, although he felt old every time he put on his reading glasses.

There was no use trying to return fire. A fast-moving, high-altitude target meant Nash would have better chance of shooting the moon.

Sticking his head out the driver's window, Nash yelled, "I'm trying to be enlightened!" Lowering his tone to almost a mumble, he added, "You big helicopter twat."

Nash had to concede his outburst had likely done little to dissuade his adversary. It had made him feel marginally better, though.

Taking advantage of the straight stretch of road and the break in fire, Nash pressed a button on his phone. "Dial Boss Man."

He put the phone on speaker. The call eventually connected.

"Do you know what time it is?" Paul's voice was groggy.

"Yes, phones have clocks now. Quite the innovation."

"Funny."

A faint voice in the background said, "Who the feckin' hell is calling you before dawn's crack?"

"Sorry Nance, go back to sleep, my love. Work." There was rustling, which Nash assumed was Paul getting out of bed and changing rooms. "What's up?"

Before Nash could answer, the Cobra rose above a hill ahead of him and opened fire. The pilot was damn good. *How the hell did he get there so fast?*

Front on, Nash could see the camouflaged gun barrels disguised as strut fairings. He was thankful it wasn't armed with hellfire missiles, though he really shouldn't exclude the possibility, especially given the day he'd had.

The Cobra's bullets pockmarked the road and headed straight at him.

"Is that..." Paul started. "Is that gunfire?"

Nash yanked the wheel to avoid the strafe of bullets and was only partially successful. Bullets ripped into the passenger side, one obliterating the headrest. Hurtling blindly down an adjacent side road, Nash did his best to keep trees between him and his fast-moving foe.

Nash yelled to be heard over the wind ripping through the pockmarked car. "Want to hear a funny story?"

THREE

"Is this going to work?"

"Probably." Paul's voice was less convinced than Nash's, and that was an extremely low bar to begin with.

Their plan had been created in around twenty seconds and under fire. Nash was in no position to offer a better solution; he was too busy trying to stay on the narrow roads while driving at breakneck speeds and trying to avoid a 20-millimetre cannon round up his arse.

The Cobra held back as he passed through whatever the hell town he was speeding through, but he suspected as soon as he hurtled past its outskirts the helicopter would be on him once more. The idea of stopping in town and taking cover was appealing, but it would likely prompt the Cobra to open fire, and the probability of civilian casualties kept Nash's foot firmly planted on the accelerator.

"How far?" Nash heard the strain in his own voice.

"Best estimate is five minutes."

Nash gulped. Five minutes was an eternity. Especially when he saw the town's buildings steadily reduce in the near distance, indicating he was about to hit open road. Five minutes was going to be five minutes too long.

"This isn't exactly what I expected to be doing when I got up in the morning."

Paul chuckled. "Funny, it's exactly what I expected when you got me out of bed this morning."

Nash knew his old friend was trying to keep the mood light, but given the circumstances it was impossible at best. He caught a flickering glimpse of a sign as he flew through the outskirts of the town.

"Sunhill. I'm just about to leave Sunhill."

There was a pause at Paul's end. "Right. You're almost there. Punch it, don't give them a straight shot."

"I wasn't planning to." Nash inhaled. "Here we go."

The town dropped away and on cue the Cobra dipped and closed the gap on the winding single carriageway. The road was thankfully tree-lined, at least for now, making the Cobra's attack vector more difficult, but certainly still within the bounds of probability. *Stupid probability.*

Nash gunned it.

Losing sight of the Cobra, he kept one eye on the blurred road, the other scanning the sky. He could hear the chopper slashing the cold night air, but couldn't see it. The sound bounced off a nearby hill, making it difficult to get a concrete fix on its ever-changing position.

The first blue sign told him his destination was coming up: Royal Air Force Fairford. The airspace was restricted. Only a madman would fly a helicopter into restricted military airspace.

At least, that was the hope.

Just as he was feeling the first inklings of relief, Nash's optimism was dashed. Instead of seeing the welcoming gates of the RAF base in the distance, he saw the black silhouette of an attack helicopter hovering directly in front of him on a straight stretch of road.

The Cobra opened fire.

Nash had run out of moves.

There was nowhere he could go.

This was it.

The bullets tore up the road in front of him, then shredded the Land Rover. Metal and plastic exploded into millions of fragments as Nash lifted his arms in a futile attempt to protect himself.

The Land Rover turned violently, lost a front wheel and tumbled out of control. The airbag deployed as Nash's world flipped end over end. Glass, metal and earth became one as the seatbelt clenched into his ragdoll body. His head slammed into the seat and god knew what else.

He blacked out.

FUGUE STATE LIFTING, Nash opened his bleary eyes. The Land Rover hissed, moaned and crackled in its post-crash death throes. Somehow, he'd landed the right way up on an embankment.

Everything hurt.

Touching his head, thick blood covered his hand. He saw flashes of light. His breathing was laboured, and his chest ached. White powder covered anything that wasn't stained with copious amounts of blood. His blood. It was everywhere. He'd have to stem the flow or the loss would render him unable to function. He had no idea where his guns were.

Wheezing, his hand fumbled with the seatbelt release. It was as if his fingers were limp sausages at the ends of his trembling hand. When he finally managed to undo the seatbelt, the door steadfastly refused to budge, no matter how hard he shouldered it.

More flashes.

It took a while for Nash to realise the lights weren't the Cobra's gunfire, nor the tumbling light of the crash. They were something else entirely.

Police lights.

Four police vehicles converged on his position. Within seconds a plump sergeant stuck her head through Nash's smashed window.

"You alright, mate?"

Ten minutes later, Nash had been cut free and sat on the back seat of a police car under his second thermal blanket of the evening, holding a weak tea. The police had cordoned off the roadway and were conducting post-accident protocols.

"I honestly don't know you survived that." A young constable shook his head. "It's a bleedin' miracle, it is, sir."

"I don't believe in miracles."

The constable let out a low whistle and motioned towards the crash site. "What would you call this then?"

"Poor driving?"

Shaking his head once more, the constable wandered off to join his compatriots, trying to clear the road of the carnage Nash had created.

The sergeant who had first addressed him strode over. Giving her a weak wave, Nash asked, "You lot from the base?"

"Correct, sir."

"Couldn't you have scrambled jets or something? I nearly didn't make it."

"Mate, Fairford is a standby airfield, not in everyday

use. We occasionally see a US heavy bomber or two, but it's not like we have a fuelled fighter jet on standby in case some idiot is getting chased by a helicopter in the middle of the night. I know it seems like an oversight on our behalf, but I'll run it by the base commander and see what she thinks."

Her language notwithstanding, Nash liked her. She wasn't easily rattled and was unafraid to speak her mind. "Quite narky in the morning, aren't we?"

The sergeant grunted. "It's four o'clock in the fucken' morning, sir, if you'll excuse the language. I was called out of bed by a screaming Home Secretary—not an underling, the actual Home Secretary—and spent all my time racing here trying to zip my pants up. If I wasn't narky I'd assume I was suffering from some sort of mental disorder."

Nash laughed, and then winced. His ribs ached like a bitch. He already had a purple sash of a bruise across his chest where the seatbelt had saved his life. Not that he was complaining. Anything was a bonus compared to where he'd recently thought he'd end up. The young constable had called it a miracle; perhaps he had dismissed the suggestion too soon.

"I'm wondering, sir, just why a local school teacher would be chased by a so-called camouflaged gunship, and how he has the ear of the Home Secretary?"

"It's a really good question." Nash let the eddies of silence swirl around them.

Seemingly annoyed at the non-answer, she went on. "Who were the mob that attacked you and terrified every resident between here and Basingstoke? This isn't some random farmer drunkenly shooting off his shotgun in the middle of the night. This was a military grade assault on my turf. Many people could have died tonight. Look at the holes in that road! I want to know who the hell shot up your car and half the bleedin' Cotswolds, and I want to know now!"

"I imagine you would."

The sergeant seethed. She sucked in air and exhaled loudly, sending vapour into the cold night air. On receiving no further reply, she screwed up her face, realising he was as closed as a padlocked book. Between gritted teeth, she said, "We're sending you up to Fairfield General for an assessment."

Nash nodded. He didn't think anything was broken, but he wasn't about to take the chance. He'd long ago dispensed with the outdated macho attitude of avoiding medical care at all costs. A post-mission check-up could save long-term damage, or even a life. His old career had taught him that, and there'd been enough instances to reinforce the lesson if he ever forgot. Rotating his shoulder joint, the old career didn't seem so old.

"Sir," the young constable approached and thumbed the wreck of the Land Rover behind him, "is there anything from the vehicle you wish to retrieve?"

Nash thought of the Heckler & Koch semiautomatics he hadn't exactly registered. He thought it best not to mention them; he'd just have to hope they'd been thrown loose by the crash.

"There's a laptop in the glove box. If it survived I'd like it returned, please." The two police officers gave him curious looks. He added, "Family photos. Sentimental, you understand?"

He was sure neither bought it, but five minutes later, the constable handed over the laptop. It was intact, though it was smeared with dirt; it must have been ejected by the collision.

If he were still a member of MI6, not reporting the laptop would be a gross violation of protocol.

But he wasn't a member of MI6. Not anymore.

There was something Nash *was*, however: hunted.

And he intended to use the laptop to find out who his hunters were. Then, he would return the favour.

"You look like ten kinds of shit."

Nash hobbled into the open-plan loft and growled. "I've missed you too."

He'd met Harriet "Harry" Gorton through a previous—albeit brief—career. Once he'd left the service, Nash had tried his hand at private investigation, but soon discovered it was nothing like Chandler or Hammett novels. Most of his cases were finding "lost" daughters shacked up with aimless losers ten years their senior, adultery, or his least favourite and most common: insurance investigations. After coming to the ugly realisation that the bulk of his work would be insurance fraud drudge work for multinational conglomerates, he'd taken a pair of scissors to his licence in disgust. He wasn't one for fighting on the wrong side.

Harry still laughed when she reminded him of the time he'd tried to educate the CEO of Aviva Insurance about the spiritual teachings of the guru of modern yoga, Ram Dass. It hadn't ended well.

His brief stint as a private detective wasn't all bad, though. At least he'd met Harry. She'd helped him on countless occasions, as her unique skill set augmented his own distinctive one. Plus, Harry's lack of legal or moral boundaries had come in useful on occasion.

Middle-aged, she had a Joan Jett punk edge about her. If half the stories she'd told Nash were even remotely true, she'd lived a hell of a life. He always looked forward to catching up with the nefarious investigator.

Her place of work was also her apartment, situated in London's trendy Hackney Wick. Filled with sixties pop art furnishings, full-scale collectables and a gaudy seventies bar at one end, it wasn't exactly subtle. The light-filled apartment occupied the entire top floor of a converted wool factory and overlooked the Lee Navigation canal. Harry's elite services had afforded her the ability to enjoy the finer things in life.

Handing Nash a chai tea without asking, she guided him to a bright red couch that would have been at home in Andy Warhol's lounge room. They made polite small talk while Nash did his best not to wince every time he inhaled. Everything still ached. After the attacks two days before, he'd given himself time to heal. And after that ten-minute break he'd gotten to work.

"So," Harry placed her no-doubt antique cup on her designer coffee table, "I'm guessing from your banged-up appearance and unannounced visit, there's something you need from me?"

Nash gave her a crooked grin. "Can't old friends just catch up?"

"Absolutely, my door's always open to you, my love, you know that." She tilted her head. "So what do you need?"

He described his recent encounters with assassins and attack helicopters. To her credit, Harry didn't react, taking the information in her stride. The woman was virtually immune to being rattled. It was another reason he liked her.

From his backpack, Nash handed over the pilfered laptop.

Turning it end over end, Harry inspected the hinge. "Is this grass?"

"I've had an intense few days. Could you..." He motioned to the device.

Harry went to open the laptop and Nash placed his hand over it. "I merely entered the house where this was located and they sent an attack helicopter after me. I suggest you don't link it to a network, wi-fi, anything. It may be my paranoia, but let's assume it's liable to go boom."

Harry frowned, acknowledging the warning. "Metaphorically or physically?"

"Yes."

"Okay. I can deep dish this thing just to be sure."

"I have no idea what that means."

"I know." She chortled. "Follow me."

Doing exactly that, down a wrought-iron spiral staircase to the floor below, Nash was confronted with server racks, computers and diagnostic equipment he couldn't even fathom the function of. In all the time he'd known her, Nash had never been inside Harry's inner sanctum.

At the far end, Nash spied a clear plastic box covering a metal stricture with various cables inside. Lifting the front of the box vertically, Harry placed the laptop inside and plugged in two cables. "It's a faraday cage, of sorts. Prevents any signal escaping, but allows me access. It should get us in."

Nash leaned forward and watched. He was reasonably computer literate, but compared to Harry he was banging rocks together in a cave while she was floating somewhere in a space station.

Closing the cover, she went to a nearby workstation and activated various programs. While she used her mouse to navigate, she addressed Nash without looking in his direction.

"So, who's trying to kill you... this time?"

There was no holding back with Harry. He trusted her implicitly. One of the few on the planet he did.

"I actually have no idea... this time. Literally none. And you know how many people I've crossed over the years."

"So many."

He nodded even though she wasn't looking. "But that's in the deep dark past, surely. I teach history now. I'm no longer in the game. A pacifist. I'm no threat to anyone."

"Someone begs to differ." Harry's eyes narrowed. "Okay, so no boom here. It's just a standard laptop, nothing special."

"Who owns it? Who tried to kill—"

"Steady on, cowboy. It's a normal laptop, it doesn't mean there's a Word document on the desktop detailing who the bad guys are and their home address. Let me do my thing."

"Sorry. It's just..."

"You haven't had anyone kill you for a while, and I know you're against all that shit now. I get it."

It was a timely reminder of why he and Harry were friends. She not only understood the spiritual journey he'd embarked on, but supported it. Although it seemed he wasn't on the straightest path to enlightenment at the moment.

She clicked, typed and squinted for several minutes. Eventually, Harry straightened her back. "Okay, so it might be a regular computer but these guys aren't lax when it comes to security."

"That...doesn't sound promising."

Harry held a finger aloft. "They've taken some good defensive measures, followed all the right protocols. There's a messaging system installed."

"Can we—"

"But it's encrypted."

"Well, can you, um, you know," Nash waved his hand at the cage, "unencrypt it or whatever?"

"It has a two hundred and fifty-six bit encryption key."

Nash gave a half shake of his head, confused.

With a sigh, Harry went on. "A two hundred and fifty-six bit key can have two to the power of two hundred and fifty-six possible combinations. Today's best supercomputers could crack it—"

"Well then..."

"—in, oh, let's say six point four quadrillion years."

Nash stared at her, open mouthed. "That's probably more time than I have."

Harry squinted. "All your passwords are the word 'password', aren't they?"

"Not all, no."

Shaking her head, Harry clicked and typed for a few more minutes. "Okay, we might have found a thing..." She glared intently at the screen. "The laptop wasn't shut down, it was just in sleep mode. So there may be data of some description in the cache copy file. Let me..." She poked her tongue out and typed some more.

Nash wasn't about to interrupt her. He felt cold. After running on nothing but adrenaline for days, he suddenly felt his age. Tired and wired at the same time, the room swayed ever so slightly. But he wasn't about to let exhaustion win. Not now.

"Okay, so it looks like whoever this belonged to was

writing an email. Whatever they wrote the draft on is gone and we can't get into the messaging program, but they copied something from a draft, so we have a fragment of it, here. Does this make any sense to you?"

Nash leaned in and read the draft text. It was only a fragment of a paragraph. Most of it made no sense, as he had no context, but on the third line he inhaled sharply and reeled back.

There was a name. One Nash knew well. It was from his time in the service, someone he'd met under fire. A name he'd thought he'd never come across again. For all sorts of reasons.

CHAPTER
FOUR

SIX YEARS BEFORE

AL HUDAYDAH

YEMEN

The rocket landed a block away with a deafening explosion. Outside, the screams of terror mingled with screams of pain. There was a lot of screaming.

"Just another day in the Service, eh?"

Jack Pinchot handed Nash a tin cup as they peered past a tattered curtain to the mayhem below. From their top-floor position, they could see that the streets below were in chaos.

Nash tasted the vile concoction and made a face. "Is there a course at Langley where they teach you how to make the worst coffee imaginable?"

"Oh sure, same class as waterboarding."

Looking at the man straight-faced, Nash replied, "I honestly believe that."

He'd met Pinchot two days before. They'd made their way into a city under siege. Al Hudaydah had been under attack from a Saudi-backed coalition several days before, putting the joint CIA/MI6 mission in doubt. Both men had lobbied their organisations to proceed as planned. The mission was too important to let something as trivial as a civil war get in the way. Their arguments worked.

Nash was thankful his last mission for MI6 hadn't been pulled from under his feet. At the same time, he was glad to finally be getting out. He was becoming jaded. He'd steadily grown frustrated at MI6's decline from the powerful organisation it had once been. The bureaucrats had taken over, more concerned with toadying up to the party in power than conducting effective spy work. Plus, his reflexes weren't what they used to be. Nash was leaving because neither he nor MI6 were making a positive difference in the world.

Nash's farewell drinks were a week from Thursday. If he lived that long. Another explosion rocked the tiny abandoned shack, covering them all in dust.

Of the team of four, Nash had worked with only one before. Marcus Hearn had been tech backup on several clandestine MI6 missions, although Nash hadn't worked with him under fire before. So far, Hearn handled himself well, offering good advice where required. Pinchot's American offsider, Travis, was another matter. Besides a grunt on their first introduction, the big man had been virtually silent for two days, either sitting up the back of the room cleaning weapons, standing guard or sleeping. He'd been so quiet Nash didn't know if Travis was his first name or last.

All four of them were filthy and malodourous. They hadn't washed in days, all sported beards of varying length and each showed the wear of perpetual stress. They were wound tight, but remained professional and at the ready. Nash wondered how long that would last.

They were holed up two hundred metres from their ultimate target, a high-walled compound allegedly defended by armed guards, security cameras, boobytraps, landmines and crocodiles—at least, according to the locals. Their various reconnoitres over the previous days had found truth in the guards and cameras, but failed to find evidence of crocodiles. Given their target, they hadn't excluded the possibility.

Abdo Qasim was a Yemen-born businessman/terrorist responsible for the downing of Singapore Airlines flight SQ 8301 out of Athens, which had killed three hundred and eleven people. The fact that one was a British cabinet official, Gareth Lowndes, made it supremely personal for MI6. The CIA had taken a vested interest because the USA's entire women's soccer team had also been killed. Their combined mission was extraction if practical; if not, they had a different set of instructions.

Qasim never showed his face in public. Thanks to an ill-advised address by the White House press secretary, he knew he was now one of the world's most wanted men. Previously he'd kept a low profile, but now he was hunkered down like a reclusive hermit with a severe case of agoraphobia. Even as the civil war encroached ever closer, he and his protectors remained securely ensconced in their fortified stronghold rather than venture out into the big bad world.

Nash put down his binoculars and rubbed his eyes. As focused as he was on the mission, he was thankful it would be his last. A new path would be forged after he returned home; he just had to get there first.

Pinchot sat next to him and handed Nash a ration pack. As he unwrapped it, Nash asked, "Have you ever dabbled in Eastern thinking?"

Instead of being surprised by the question, Pinchot looked thoughtful. He replied, "I did tai chi once."

"And?"

Pinchot smiled. "I've been on twenty-seven foreign deployments; not a scratch, not one. One morning of tai chi and I pulled my back and couldn't walk for two days." He paused. "Why do you ask?"

"Just something I've been mulling over, you know. Nothing major, just a complete philosophical change in my core principles and beliefs. Nothing difficult."

"Sounds... challenging."

"I imagine it will be."

Nash laughed and took a bite out of the ration pack. It tasted like cardboard that had once been waved in the general vicinity of some roast beef.

He took a swig of water to get rid of the taste, then took up the binoculars again to take in the compound. "We're going to have to go in, aren't we?"

"I told you that yesterday." It was a matter-of-fact comment, not a pointed one.

Turning to Pinchot, Nash said, "Get word to your inside man, he'd better prepare for our arrival."

Marcus Hearn's leg jiggled. "So when do we go?"

At the same time Pinchot and Nash replied, "Tonight."

Hearn exhaled loudly, trepidation smacked across his face. "Great."

Travis remained mute on the matter.

~

THERE WAS no need to cut the power. There was none.

The city had been without power since forces hit the outskirts of the city and began their attack. Streets were filled with fleeing citizens, pro-Iranian or pro-Saudi Yemen forces, and anyone else stuck in the middle. Fires raged in different zones. Chaos didn't even begin to describe it.

Even at 2 am the streets were filled with desperate people making desperate moves. Panic was as thick as the incessant smoke.

Standing in a dusty, hooded robe, Nash nervously checked his watch for the seventieth time. No matter how many missions he'd been on, he always got nervous. Instead of fighting it, he welcomed it. It meant he was still human. Only a psychopath or automaton wouldn't feel some trepidation before an assault. It didn't mean Nash wasn't ready. He had to be, or he and his team would likely die.

Watching the side entrance of Qasim's compound from his position across the street, Nash clung to the shadows. In spite of the turmoil on the streets, the guards kept their regular patrols along the outer walls. That meant they were disciplined, well-trained and professional.

They kept to their established sentry schedule. Everything seemed routine. That didn't make Nash any less nervous.

He checked his watch again.

Had the minute hand gone backwards? *Breathe.* He stretched his neck from side to side.

The comms piece in Nash's ear clicked. "Inside man has given us a go." Pinchot's voice was calm. "Repeat, inside man has given us a go, over."

"Acknowledged."

Nash stepped out from the shadows and crossed the street. At the far end, a cart rounded the corner, dragged by two men who clearly wanted to be anywhere else in the world. That indicated they weren't stupid. The cart held a woman, two small children and seemingly all their worldly possessions. Nash dodged the cart and made his way along the fortress wall.

Without breaking stride, he extracted a black plastic box and peeled off the adhesive strip on one side. As he strode past the heavy wooden door, Nash quickly placed the device above the door handle and walked on.

Maintaining his pace as to not arouse suspicion, he spoke into his comms. "One minute. Check in."

"Pinchot, ready."

"Hearn, ready."

There was a pause. Eventually, "Travis, ready."

The man's voice was higher than Nash had expected.

Nash reached the corner and turned. The street wasn't clear. The cart he'd passed had halted in the middle of the street, directly across from the door and the explosive charge he'd set. One of the men leaned down and massaged his calf. The family group were engaged in casual chit chat.

Under his breath, Nash muttered, "Move, you bastard. *Move.*"

"What's that?"

As quietly as he could, Nash replied, "We have civilians in the blast radius."

"Ignore them, they're not going to last long in this city anyway." Pinchot's voice was even. "Stay on mission, Nash."

"We need to abort."

"Negative, our man says it's now or never. We're not going to get another shot at this."

His body felt like it was on fire. He was sweating despite the chilly night air.

"Nash." Pinchot's voice broke. "Leave them. Don't—"

Nash broke into a run. Sidling up to the two surprised men, he asked, "Hal tahtaj musaeadatan?"

Without waiting for a response, he picked up the handle of the cart and grinned inanely as he heaved the vehicle forward. The two reluctant and wary men had no choice but to join him. The cart rolled forward while the older man who had halted them hobbled along, doing his best to keep pace.

Moving steadily faster, the men's faces grew more concerned, but they were too busy trying to keep up with Nash's ever-increasing pace, so their concerns remained unspoken. They were virtually at a run when they reached the end of the street and the corner of the compound.

Extracting himself from the cart, Nash gave them a wave. "Adhhab mae allah!"

As the baffled cart occupants rounded the corner, the explosion ripped apart the night and the door. The citizens of Al Hudaydah were not done with their screaming just yet.

Retracing his steps, Nash raced towards the now-burning cinders of the door. Extracting his MI6-issued Browning Hi-Power, he leapt through the breach.

His first shot took out a guard high on the walkway surrounding the compound. The guard's momentary hesitation cost him his life. The silencer muffled the shot, but the element of surprise would soon evaporate and be replaced by a rallying defence. They had to achieve their goal before that happened.

Pistol raised, Nash made his way deeper into the compound. Two more guards. Two more shots. Two more deaths.

Security didn't seem as well trained as he'd thought, or perhaps they hadn't been warned that intruders had breached the compound. Nash suspected it was the latter. Unless given express instructions, guards don't generally like to fire weapons within their own stronghold.

Reaching a small courtyard, Nash heard a bird call from behind. He swivelled, gun raised. Pinchot emerged from the darkness, his own gun high.

"You're a fucking bleeding heart, you are."

Nash shrugged. "What are we in this for if not to protect the innocent?"

"In case you missed it, there's a war raging in this city. That family you so bravely saved aren't going to last the night." Pinchot sniffed, keeping his voice low. "I didn't think there were any idealists left in the world."

Checking all corners of the courtyard for approaching enemy, Nash said, "Speaking of idealists, where's your inside man?"

Pinchot jerked his head to the left. "This way."

The two men worked in sync, covering one another as they made their way further inside the enemy compound. The occasional burst of gunfire told them Travis and Hearn were performing their task of distraction admirably.

Nash led them to a first-floor room separate from the main house, Pinchot charged behind him up the stairs. The single petrified-looking guard didn't even make a full turn before Pinchot put a bullet in his head and he slumped to the ground.

Surging forward, Pinchot shot out the lock on the door and kicked it in. They both burst in. A dishevelled white male in shorts and a Dallas Cowboys t-shirt spun around in shock.

"Holy shit! Don't you people knock? I nearly shit myself."

In Nash's opinion, Tyler Sikes was an idiot. A naive romanticist, sure, but still an idiot. The American hacker had somehow been recruited by Qasim under the misapprehension he would be fighting for environmental causes. By the time he realised Qasim's goals were unaligned to his own, it was too late. He'd been forced to support Qasim's plan's for global disruption.

The man certainly wasn't the technical definition of an idiot. In fact, he was closer to a genius. He had five degrees by the time he was twenty, and by the time he was old enough to drink he was being pursued by every leading corporation and government organisation. He could have achieved so much.

Several weeks earlier, Sikes had managed to reach out to the CIA to plead his case. This was where Pinchot came in. Five Eyes alerted the CIA to an MI6 operation to extract Qasim that was already underway, led by Nash. The organisations combined their efforts. Pinchot had been receiving regular messages from Sikes, replete with regret and pleas to make amends. Nash had his doubts. It was unlikely flight SQ 8301 would have been downed if not for Sikes' assistance. The man had confessed to altering passenger manifests to allow Qasim's men to hijack the plane and crash it into the Bay of Bengal. Coerced or not, Sikes had blood on his hands. Nash still believed the man was an idiot, and potentially something far worse.

"Where's Qasim?" There was an edge to Pinchot's voice.

"No small talk, then?" Sikes smiled, but it was all bluster. The man was terrified. "Nice to meet you too, Pinchot. Just so you know, I like to be wined and dined before—"

"Shut it." Pinchot stepped forward. Every muscle in his body was taut. He was wound far tighter than Nash had realised. "Where the fuck is he?"

Sikes' terror multiplied. He gulped. "Like, uh, they've kept me under house arrest since the rebels hit the outskirts. I... I don't know."

"The fuck?" Pinchot grabbed the man by the front of his stained t-shirt and slammed him into the wall. "You said it was now or never. You said you knew where he was!"

"Would you have come for me if I hadn't?"

Everyone in the room knew the answer to the question.

Before Pinchot could reply, their earpieces buzzed. "We're under heavy fire, south corner. Repeat, we're under fire. Need urgent assistance. Respond."

Hearn's voice was strained. The diversion he and Travis had provided had been turned against them.

Pinchot and Nash exchanged looks. A wordless conversation took place. With no exact lock on Qasim, they would lose precious minutes searching the vast compound, and Travis and Hearn, now under fire, could offer no support. Now that the guards were alert to their presence, their offensive position would soon turn to one of defence, if it hadn't already. Qasim would dig in and fight to the last man. They'd lost the element of surprise.

Pinchot punched the wall next to Sikes' head. He pressed the button on his neck for comms. "Abort. Repeat, abort, abort, abort."

"Roger. Bugging out. Over."

Pinchot and Nash raced for the door, their raised pistols at the ready.

"What about me?"

They turned to Sikes, who was clearly close to shitting himself—literally. Abdo Qasim would soon discover Sikes' betrayal, if he hadn't already. If left behind, the American's short-lived fate would be one of pain and suffering.

Nash cast his gaze to a square-jawed Pinchot. It was obvious there was a battle waging behind his eyes.

Between clenched teeth, the CIA agent growled, "Follow us, keep your head down and we'll see."

The slightest glimpse of relief washed across Sikes' face. "Do I get a gun?"

As one, Pinchot and Nash replied, "No."

The trio made their way back the way they'd come. The two guards they encountered were quickly dispatched. In seconds they were back on the street and running for their lives. They made their way to the safe house unscathed, where they were met by Travis and Hearn. The latter sported a bloody arm, but was grateful to be out of the firefight.

Before they had a chance to debrief, Pinchot roared in anger and proceeded to destroy the makeshift kitchen with the butt of his M4 carbine. Sikes backed into a wall in horror. It was plain Hearn and Travis could sympathise, and they left Pinchot to his rage. Nash took the rickety wooden ladder to the roof.

From one of the highest vantage points in the town, Nash was able to see the compound from which they'd just escaped. Inside Qasim's secluded oasis, machine-gun fire lit up the sky. Victory fire, no doubt celebrating the triumph over the Western intruders.

Through his scope, Nash saw a bearded, white-robed man emerge smoking a fat cigar. One of Qasim's men handed the reclusive leader a machine gun and he joined his guards in their triumphant fire.

Nash exhaled slowly and pulled the trigger of his sniper's rifle. Qasim's head exploded in a burst of blood, bone and brain.

"Nice shot."

Nash spun to see Pinchot standing behind him, seemingly a completely different man to the one who'd been engulfed in rage only moments before.

"That's it. My last kill. I'm done now."

"You really getting out?"

Nash pulled the bolt to extract the cartridge from the chamber and started the process of disassembling the rifle. After his previous mission in Bolivia, he realised he'd seen too much. He'd *done* too much. Nash had to get out before he was consumed by violence. If that happened, there would be no coming back. Bolivia had showed him just how close he was to that void. On that fateful mission, he'd almost taken a step down the path to becoming the very thing he most abhorred. Instead, he chose a different path. It was why he was stepping back now—because if he didn't, Nash feared he'd never find his way back. The execution of Qasim was also the termination of his violent days. The bloody end to a murderous story.

The CIA agent gave an approximation of a smirk. "I guess we call this one last mission accomplished, then?"

Nash had never needed a drink more in his life. "We do. Not pretty, but we got there."

"We're not done yet." Pinchot growled. "We need to get out of this stinking country first." He nodded towards the compound. "And I'd suggest we do so rather quickly".

Not about to argue, Nash stood, leaving the sniper rifle behind. "Agreed."

It took them less than five minutes to collect their packs and make their way out of a side entrance. The four spies and Sikes piled into one of the few remaining functioning cars in the city, a beaten-up Toyota Yaris that looked ready to fall apart at any moment. They remained mute for a good ten minutes before they reached the outskirts of the city, the opposite side from the encroaching war. Joining a convoy of refugees, they kept pace with the slow-moving evacuees until dawn.

On reaching Al-Jamadi they broke off from the convoy and drove to an abandoned parking lot where two identical Toyota Hilux's awaited them. Their Yaris spluttered and made a death rattle, its final act now done. Without a word being spoken, the spies started to load their gear into the two separate vehicles. Hearn and Nash loaded one Hilux, Pinchot and Travis the other.

Stretching his legs after the long car journey, Sikes asked, "Which team do I go with?"

Nash and Pinchot exchanged glances. The latter answered first.

"Neither."

Jaw dropped, Sikes' voice went three octaves higher. "What? I gave you all the information! I told you exactly where he was. You wouldn't have found him without me!"

"You didn't tell us *exactly* where he was, just a general location." Pinchot rocked on his heels. "Most importantly, you helped them blow up a plane. Sure, you didn't press the button, but you used your hacking skills to allow others to do just that. Those murders are on you."

"I didn't! I didn't know!" The man was truly panicked

now. "I thought I was going to be an environmental terrorist."

"See," Nash shook his head, "I know you think that's better, but there's still terrorist in the title."

"You can't leave me in this goddam country. I'll die. I don't have money, a passport, anything."

"You have your charming personality." There was no humour in Pinchot's tone. "I wish you luck with that."

Sikes' desperation was now mingling with anger. "You may as well have left me to die back there."

Nash sighed. "Listen. We're going to tell our respective governments you *did* die back there. Not many people in life get a second chance, Sikes. This is yours. The four of us are the only ones who know you lived. If you make it out of here, you've earned that second chance. Good luck."

All four intelligence agents went back to their tasks, ignoring him. Travis and Hearn gave the other two men a nod of thanks before getting into the passenger sides of their respective cars.

It was always difficult to find the right words when you had served under fire with another human being. The bond forged was simply beyond words. Nash and Pinchot realised it, and didn't try.

"Mason."

"Jack."

The men shook hands. After the brevity of farewells, each man walked to his vehicle and started it up.

As the sun rose, bathing everything in a sea of orange, it wasn't the only act of dawning. Sikes was in a state of frantic terror as the gravity of his situation struck him. He hopped from foot to foot, running his hands through his greasy hair.

Throat constricted by dread, he addressed Nash. "What, what do I do?"

Nash wound down his window. "If you survive, make something of your life. Make it count."

The words did nothing to dispel the panic in Sikes' eyes. He realised he was being left for dead and no platitudes would change that fact.

Nash wound up his window and the vehicles took separate paths.

CHAPTER
FIVE

PRESENT

Harry leaned forward on her bright red couch.
"That's a hell of a story."

"And classified. I trust it never leaves this room?"

Harry glared at Nash like he'd asked the stupidest question in the history of mankind. She tapped away at her laptop. The woman was never more than a few paces from a computer of some description.

"After that, I think you need a drink." She stood and slipped behind her bar, taking her laptop with her. "I know I do. What can I get you?"

After recounting his Yemen mission, he decided it wasn't the worst idea he'd ever heard. "Whiskey sour?"

Harry rolled her eyes. "You're such an old man."

Mixing his drink, Harry made herself an elderflower

spritz with exotic ingredients Nash could only guess at. They sat at the bright orange bar and toasted nothing in particular.

The name on the message fragment from the pilfered laptop was Tyler Sikes. The man he'd left in a tiny Yemen village without water, supplies or money. The man they'd literally left for dead.

Yet, somehow, he hadn't died. And given that the email had referred to him in the present tense, evidently he'd done more than simply survive.

Harry took a sip of her cocktail. "So, the guy you saved is now trying to kill you?"

"Well, saved *then* abandoned, but yes, it seems that way." He sighed. "I would have thought a Christmas card would have been enough."

Nash recalled the expression on the man's face as the cars drove away. It must have truly seemed like they'd left him to die. Would that be reason enough to send armed assassins and gunships years after the fact? It was such a disproportionate response Nash had a hard time buying it. Overkill didn't even come close. Not to mention how the then-penniless hacker could have accumulated the funds for such activities. It didn't ring true.

Nash scratched the back of his head and sipped his drink.

"Why'd you save him?"

Nash turned to Harry, surprised. "What's that?"

"Sikes. Why did you save him in the first place? The guy helped a terrorist. Coerced or not, he did it. You could have left him in that terrorist's compound and been done with it. But you didn't. Those ethics of yours seem to have come back and bitten you on the arse, wouldn't you say?"

Nash couldn't argue that one. It was a running joke that

he'd never cut it as a private detective because his morals kept getting in the way. He and Harry had had countless discussions about him struggling with the moral implications of unearthing adultery or someone scamming a couple of hundred pounds from an evil multinational insurance company. It never really sat well with him. Mason Nash wasn't a take the money and run sort.

"Well, Pinchot didn't leave him in the compound either."

"That's not what I asked. I asked why *you* didn't." Harry raised a challenging eyebrow.

While he loved that he and Harry had a close relationship, it could be damned annoying at times. He chose not to answer. Mainly because he didn't have a definitive answer. Or even a smartarsed one.

"You still in contact with Jack Pinchot?" Harry seemed as unable to drop the subject as Nash was. "Maybe he could use the CIA to get a handle on Sikes."

Nash eyed Harry sideways. "I would have thought you'd be all over this one."

Harry flicked her thumb towards her laptop. "The search began compiling the second you told me the story." She leaned in and checked the screen. "So far nothing for Sikes. That, in itself, strikes me as weird. Like, there's no mention of him *at all*. No missing person reference, nothing. I've been at this a long time, Nash, and no one just disappears."

"Not without help."

Harry tapped her nose. "Not without help. I'm thinking maybe your mate could leverage a few databases I don't currently have access to."

Frowning in agreement, Nash balled his fists. Twice

he'd been caught by surprise, on the back foot and unpre-pared. He wasn't about to allow a third.

"I can try to reach out to Pinchot. Maybe the CIA have info on Sikes; he was a Yank, after all." Stretching his hands above his head, he grunted as he remembered his bruised ribs. "But getting hold of Pinchot might be a challenge in itself. It's not like secret service agents hand out business cards."

Writing a note on a post-it note, Harry passed it to him. "Here's his mobile number—sorry, cell number. Bloody Yanks."

"You are a resourceful individual, Harry."

"You don't pay me to sit here and look pretty."

"I'm paying you?"

Harry motioned towards the piece of paper. "For that, hell yeah you are."

"Oh, right."

THE FIRST SURPRISE was when Pinchot answered the call.

The second was that he was in London.

By the time Pinchot said he was staying at the luxurious Savoy, Nash's ample supply of surprise had run out.

The fact that he was in London was... odd, although not wildly out of character. But as much as Nash attempted to rationalise Pinchot's presence, he was still on edge. Then again, right now everything put him on edge.

The prestigious Savoy was the first purpose-built luxury hotel in London. The name Savoy screamed lavish-ness and indulgence. Even after one hundred and thirty something years it is still the epitome of luxury, especially in the eyes of foreigners like Pinchot. The only thing more British would be spending the night in Buckingham Palace.

Waiting in the jet-black and gold confines of the art deco Beaufort Bar, Nash messaged Harry again. She still had no trace of Sikes' existence post-Yemen and bugger all even from before then. Harry was now operating on her own time, gratis; the mystery had intrigued her so. The latest message simply read, "How the rudding fuck does a human disappear from the internet without a trace?!?!"

Nash sent back a shrugging emoji in reply.

Nursing his rather nice Suntory old-fashioned, Nash's mind tried to process a million thoughts at once. It turned out Pinchot had left the CIA not long after Nash left MI6. He'd entered the world of "private contracting", he said, but had refused to elaborate further on the phone.

Finishing his cocktail, Nash realised he was still on guard. It may have been paranoia. Then again, it may have been legitimate guardedness. It was a mode that had served him well in the past, but one he'd hoped would remain stashed among his other weaponry in the bathroom alcove of his home. Nash eyed the room for surveillance, potential threats and escape routes. He was surprised how quickly he'd slipped on the familiar suit of espionage. And just how well it still fit.

Spotting Pinchot as soon as he entered the bar, Nash waved him over.

After a handshake, Nash jerked his thumb towards the room. "Nice digs."

"Nothing you're not familiar with from a past life, I'm sure."

The two had gotten to know each other well in the Yemen safe house. Waiting for days on end, you tended to find anything to talk about. Certain personal facts were bound to fall out. Until that moment, Nash had forgotten he'd even told Pinchot about his childhood. It was a subject he rarely spoke of. Harry knew, and a few select friends, but not many more. The fact that he'd confessed to his privileged upbringing reminded Nash of how quickly he and Pinchot had formed a bond.

They made polite small talk about the weather as Pinchot took off his coat and ordered a negroni and another old-fashioned for Nash. Nash sensed Pinchot was uncharacteristically nervous, which put Nash even more on edge. After a good ten minutes of Pinchot asking generic questions about how he was and what he'd been up to since leaving the service, Nash slapped his palm on the table, stopping Pinchot mid-sentence.

Nash let the shock of the move hover for a moment, then leaned in close. "You seem jittery, Jack." His eyes narrowed. "What's going on? Your eyes are darting about like ping pong balls in a washing machine."

Instead of taking offence, Pinchot issued a wry grin. "An old buddy pops up out of the blue, kind of takes you by surprise, that's all. You don't seem to be the epitome of calm either, old friend."

"Given that everyone I meet of late wants to kill me, you'll forgive me if I'm not particularly laid back. Assassins and gunships tend to make one a little jumpy."

Pinchot laughed hesitantly, as if he suspected Nash was joking but didn't entirely get it. Seeing the complete lack of humour in his manner, Pinchot gave a slight shake of his head.

"Those... those things didn't happen, obviously... did they?"

Nash could feel his jaw pulse.

Leaning forward, Pinchot lowered his voice. "Why did you call me, Mason?"

"Is there somewhere we can talk in private?"

Visibly confused, Pinchot gave a hint of a frown. "My room? That work?"

Leaving their half-finished drinks, Nash threw a pile of cash on the table and gestured towards the nearby lifts.

Minutes later, they entered the small but luxurious hotel room. There was a bed, a bar, a couple of comfy looking armchairs and a small glass table. Nash made Pinchot walk in front of him. He wasn't about to trust anyone, friend or not. Jacket open, Nash's shoulder holster was unclipped.

Pinchot sat at the small table and motioned for Nash to do the same. "I feel there's a story here. Let's have it."

Nash gave him the abbreviated version of the last few days, from walking into the Hangman's Inn to the police saving his arse from a helicopter gunship. He strategically left out Harry and the discovery of the laptop. In this abridged version, Nash had searched the safe house to find nothing but overnight luggage.

Pinchot did nothing but blink at him for several seconds. "I'm kind of disappointed we left those drinks now. Jesus Christ, Nash, what the fuck have you gotten yourself into?"

"That's all I've been asking myself for three days straight."

"If that story isn't an excuse to raid the mini bar I don't know what is." Pinchot shook his head in amazement as he strode towards the bar fridge. "Gunships. These pricks don't do things by halves, do they?" Taking stock of what was on offer, he asked, "Chivas?"

"Fine."

As Nash told his story he'd been gauging Pinchot's reactions, but it was hard to get a complete handle on him. It was why he'd made such a good CIA operative. While he made all the right gasps and proclamations of surprise, it was difficult to ascertain his true feelings.

That was the problem with the spy game: everyone was equally adept at deception. It made uncovering the truth a Sisyphean endeavour.

Dropping in ice from the ice bucket, Pinchot poured a bottle into each glass. Accepting his drink, Nash waited for Pinchot to return to his seat. Except he never made it that far. The gun in the back of Nash's head indicated the conversation had made a slight turn.

"Your heater, on the table." The gun was pressed harder into the back of his skull. "Two fingers on the handle, nice and slow if you don't mind."

As he did as requested, Nash said, "Did you just say heater? Who are you, James Cagney?"

"I'm thankful you're all peaceful and zen and shit now." Pinchot tapped the gun against Nash's temple. "Otherwise this would go an entirely different way."

Nash chose not to advise Pinchot that the non-violent part of him felt like it had an "out of order" sign on it. In reality, Nash was seething. And not because of the barrel pressed to the back of his head. Well, not *only* that. It wasn't exactly the first time Nash had a gun pointed at him.

It was the fact that, yet again, he found himself at the wrong end of a weapon and he still didn't know why. His long-standing pacifism wavered like it never had before. Normally, his violent past seemed like a distant fever dream, but now, long-buried instincts lashed out. It took every ounce of his strength to keep them at bay. He wasn't that man anymore, was he?

Pinchot patted him down. Satisfied Nash wasn't further armed, he pocketed Nash's Heckler & Koch and pulled up a chair so he could sit behind him. The Browning was no longer pressed against his head, but it was close enough to make the shot unmissable.

"I can only imagine what you must be thinking right now." Pinchot's tone was even.

"Me? I was wondering why soy milk and soy sauce are nothing alike."

"I…" Pinchot sighed heavily, as if realising the current situation didn't make for polite casual tête-à-tête. "How the hell did you find me?"

"I called you, you answered." Nash forced his tense shoulders to shrug, then downed the Chivas in one gulp. He assumed it wasn't poisoned. It would be a waste of scotch whisky.

"That's not what I'm asking and you know it." There was the slightest amused twinge in Pinchot's tone.

Nash didn't answer. He was angered his old colleague had chosen to pull a gun on him. Even more so because he didn't know why. Was it connected to Sikes or the attempts on his life? He had no idea. That didn't mean he wasn't going to find out.

Nash flexed and unflexed his fists. "It seems I was accurate when I said everyone I meet of late wants to kill me."

"I don't want to kill you, Mason."

"The gun in your hand says otherwise… old friend."

There was rummaging behind him; Nash assumed it was Pinchot reaching for his mobile phone. It was time to put Pinchot's claim of not wanting to kill him to the test.

With a big intake of air, Nash shoved the glass table away and rose. Pinchot's gun immediately returned to the back of his head.

"Hey, hey, stay put. Sit down, now!"

Never one for taking orders, Nash turned, and in a lightning-fast move stepped in under Pinchot's arm. At the same time he savagely twisted the gun in Pinchot's hand to the right, hearing a satisfying snap. Pinchot howled, and Nash punched him in the throat, killing the noise instantly.

The days of non-stop high adrenaline and fear manifested themselves in his fists. Punching Pinchot in the face, he bellowed, "Will", he punched his face again, "everyone," he moved to hit Pinchot's stomach, "stop", another blow, "trying," another, "to," he gave Pinchot a backhander, forcing him to stagger back, "kill," he finally pistol whipped him to the floor, "me!" Nash stepped back and inhaled unsteadily.

It was the most un-zen he'd been in years and he hated himself for it. It was a shame he couldn't get answers through meditation.

Patting down the man like Pinchot had done only a minute before, Nash took his pistol back and flexed his free hand. The former CIA operative glared up, bloodied and beaten.

"You broke my fucking finger!"

"You pulled a gun on me." Nash paced. "You're fucking lucky that's all you got."

Pinchot touched the blood trickling from his split lip, then observed his stained finger for a moment before casting his gaze towards Nash. "Aren't you meant to be a pacifist?"

"I would be if everyone would stop trying to kill me. It really fucks up my karmic alignment."

Pinchot tilted his head. "You going to kill me now?"

"Right now I'm making no promises." Nash chose a drishti, or focused gaze on a piece of the floor, used to develop concentrated intention, creating a sense with-drawal. He used the moment to centre his intent. "It all depends on how you answer my questions."

Rocking back and forth on the lush carpet, Pinchot cradled his finger. "And what if I don't want to answer any of your questions?"

Nash leaned forward, so close he could hear Pinchot's rattled breaths, and pressed the gun to his forehead. "Then you won't have to worry about a broken finger for very long."

With blood pouring from one of the wounds on his forehead, Pinchot gulped. His eyes were wide, whether from fear, shock or pain, Nash wasn't sure. Perhaps it was all of the above.

The room was no good for an interrogation. He had to get the man out of the Savoy. Far easier said than done, though. It wasn't like he could hoist him over his shoulder and carry him through reception onto a busy street in the middle of London unquestioned.

Nash pulled out his phone, keeping his eye and gun on a now-panicked Pinchot.

The call was picked up within seconds. "Hey, want to make a few thousand pounds?" Nash smiled. "Thought so. I'm going to need a few things. Got a pen?"

He looked down at his captive. As Nash rattled off his list, Pinchot looked back at him with growing fear.

CHAPTER
SIX

The knock on the door made Pinchot jump. In contrast, Nash remained perfectly still. He was still surprised at how quickly his unique set of skills came back to him. It was like they'd never left.

Not for the first time, Nash wondered what the fuck he was doing. He should have been in bed long before now. His normal night-time routine had been grading papers followed by some meditation and a good book before bed. His bedtime had been getting earlier and earlier the older he got. He'd been wanting to change it up, but this was ridiculous. He was meant to be retired. He *wanted* to be retired. Or at least, he thought he did.

This wasn't what someone his age should have been doing. Hell, at any age.

The path he had stumbled down wasn't one he ever wanted to follow. It went against everything he stood for and had been actively working towards. His counsellor may very well call it a relapse and tell him to stop. But Nash couldn't stop, not now. He had to walk this path no matter where it led him. He had to find what lay at the end.

Secured to a chair with a combination of bathrobe belts and curtain ties, Pinchot wasn't going anywhere. That didn't mean he wasn't struggling against his bonds, of course.

Leaving him to his fruitless endeavours, Nash opened the hotel room door. He was greeted by a woman dressed in a cap and oversized jacket, carrying an Uber Eats bag. Harry looked pleased with herself.

Handing over the bag, she said, "Please don't ask where I got that stuff."

"Why would I do that? You didn't ask why I needed it."

She gave a tilt of her head, acknowledging the point. "I will ask one thing, though. Why milk? Why, among all the other, ah, materials, do you need a pint of milk?"

Nash put on his best schoolboy charm and said nothing.

Realising that was all she was going to get, Harry looked past Nash to see the restrained Pinchot. She didn't bat an eyelid. "Two am?"

"Yep. That okay?"

"Already on it. See you then." She pivoted and headed towards the lifts.

Closing the door, Nash made his way back to the table and the captive Pinchot.

"What's happening at two am?"

Nash opened the paper bag and extracted a syringe. "Nothing you need to worry about."

AT THE STROKE of two the lights went out. Nash was ready. The unconscious Pinchot was slumped by the door, and the two weapons were tucked away. Nash had wiped every surface twice to ensure none of his fingerprints were present, and had used the unconscious Pinchot to make sure his were left behind. One set of prints was fine, no prints was suspicious.

Nash had observed the hotel security cameras on the way to Pinchot's room. Harry had hacked into the security system and wiped everything up to the time Nash had entered the building. It was likely the power loss would be blamed. The blackout also provided cover for Nash to carry the unconscious body down three flights of stairs unnoticed. At least, that was the theory. He was about to put the theory to the test.

The knock came at exactly five minutes past. Harry stood in a black hoodie and handed him one, too.

"But the security cameras are out?"

"Yes, but only in this building. Once you're out on the street you'll be under surveillance of some description. London is the CCTV capital of the world, remember? A hoodie gives you cover."

"You're one smart cookie, Harriet Gorton."

"Damn fuckin A, I am." She looked at the slumped body. "You ready?"

Giving her a nod, Nash hoisted Pinchot onto his shoulder. "Let's go."

Taking the lead, Harry walked ten metres ahead, watching and listening for any signs of life. They made it to the stairwell without incident. Thankfully the emergency lighting had kicked in, providing minimal illumination. Reaching the basement level, Harry went through the door first and returned moments later to give Nash the all-clear.

Halting at the street exit, Harry once again took the lead. On her signal, Nash strode onto the empty street. Harry stood beside the open boot of her black '68 Dodge

Charger and scanned the street. Nash always joked that Harry's car was inappropriate for London. She always replied with a raised middle finger. Placing Pinchot in the huge space, Nash wasn't complaining now. You could fit another five bodies in there. He closed the boot quietly.

"The bag you requested is in the back seat." Harry held the keys in front of him. "The plates are fake, so take them off when you get to where you're going. The real ones are underneath."

"Can they trace the model back to you?"

Harry shook her head. "Nah. It's registered to an old Japanese man who apparently lives in a vacant lot in North Ockendon. We're golden." As Nash reached out to take the keys, she jerked them back. "I want this baby back without a scratch, you hear me? Not a scratch."

"Cross my heart."

"And hope to die?"

"No."

"Fair enough." Harry handed him the keys. "See you after..." she flicked her thumb towards the car, "you do whatever it is you have to do."

And Nash did just that.

He drove just below the speed limit, leaving plenty of room between him and the cars in front, avoiding any potential accidents. The last thing he wanted was to explain to the police why he had a bound and unconscious man in his boot. Best to avoid that kind of awkward conversation.

He arrived at his destination at a little after three in the morning. For the last half hour, Nash hadn't seen another car on the road. It was easy to believe he was the only one awake in the whole country.

Well, except for the frantic thumping coming from the boot.

Outside, all was serene. Thick woods on all sides, the small cabin at the end of the drive the only structure to be seen. It was away from any major roads. It was secluded. It was quiet. In other words, it was perfect for Nash's needs.

Turning off the engine, Nash grabbed the duffel bag from the back seat and trod across the gravel driveway to the rear of the jet-black car. Extracting his pistol, he stood back, in case Pinchot lashed out. Nash had asked Harry to ensure there were no tyre irons or the like in the boot, just in case.

There was no need. When Nash opened the boot, Pinchot raised his bound hands defensively. The entire left side of his head was now a purple bruise. He kicked the wheel arch in anger.

Nash sighed. "The torture that awaits you in the next few hours, whatever pain you endure, will be nothing compared to what you will get if you dint this car."

Pinchot had managed to remove the gag. "Torture?" His fear only grew. "What the hell is going on, Mason? I'm your friend."

"A *friend* who pulled a gun on me."

"Don't you think this," he held up his tied hands, "is an overreaction?"

"Typical American thinking. That's why you always had such trouble with your foreign policy. You consistently ignored the possible ramifications of your actions."

"The English can talk."

"Touché."

Nash yanked Pinchot out of the car and his captive took in the surroundings. Clearly comprehending what the out-of-the-way location meant, he gulped.

"Where are we?"

Nash pushed him towards the cabin. "Somewhere secure."

"Your family estate?"

Pausing his advance, Nash gave the former CIA agent an admiring gaze. "I don't have an estate. Not anymore."

The fact Pinchot had even brought the subject up was curious. That he got it right was impressive. Nash was reminded once again of who he was dealing with. The man was just as smart and capable as he was. And just as ruthless.

Nash pushed Pinchot forward.

Half turning, Pinchot said, "Killing me isn't good for your karma, you know."

Nash unlocked the door to the cabin. "Maybe I won't kill you, who knows?" He paused. "I will make you wish you were dead, if that's any consolation."

"It's really not."

Inside the shack, the furniture was covered in sheets, and a thick layer of dust covered everything.

"I know all your tricks, Nash. This isn't going to work." While Pinchot's words were strong, the delivery left a lot to be desired.

"It might not, you're right." He motioned for Pinchot to enter the musty shack. "Either way, this is going to be very unpleasant for you."

"We're friends." There was desperation in his voice now. "How could you do this?"

"Same way you pulled a gun on me. Friendships can be fickle, can't they?" Nash pointed to a wooden chair in the middle of the room. "Shall we begin?"

Nash felt sick. He'd never enjoyed torture, no matter the subject. In flashes, he saw past victims in all their pained bloody gore. Every victim rushed towards him in a never-ending cavalcade of regret. His counsellor would have a term for it; a post-traumatic stress disorder episode. It didn't matter how many lives had been saved as a result of all the pain he'd inflicted, the fact that he'd been the instrument of such cruelty had kept him awake at night for years.

The procession of past ruthlessness had an unexpected consequence. Nash was overcome by a sense of other-worldly detachment. It was as if he was observing another man carrying out activities he'd tried to forget. It was clear it was a PTSD episode; he was dissociated from his surroundings but seemed unable to do anything about it. His body went into autopilot, and Nash's disconnected mind had no choice but to go along for the ride.

Over the next few hours it was hard to know who was the most horrified. Pinchot, at exactly how adept Nash was at brutal interrogations, or Nash, who discovered just how quickly his old vicious skill set came back to him.

There were no questions for Pinchot. Not yet. That wasn't how this worked. First, Nash had to break down his subject. Let him slowly realise how hopeless the situation was. Asking polite questions would not garner the answers he sought. No, first he had to break the man—a job made much harder due to the subject's countless years of training. Not that the task was impossible. But Pinchot would endure hours more pain and suffering than the average recipient of Nash's cruel techniques.

And hours it was.

Nash was relentless. He hardly noticed the morning sun, so focused was he on his work. He meticulously followed an established regimen he'd used countless times before. The work disgusted him and made him sick to his stomach, but he seemed completely incapable of stopping himself. He had to wonder what type of man he'd be afterward.

As a trained CIA professional, Pinchot was skilled in both the application of and defence against torture. It was, after all, part of the job. But theory was one thing, reality quite another. He'd done well to withstand Nash's brutal and inelegant torment.

For a time.

Placing the bloodied pliers on the side table, Nash picked up what until recently had been Pinchot's left first premolar. In retrospect, he wished he'd thought to organise some sand to spread on the floor. It helped soak up the blood.

Holding the tooth up to the light, Nash casually asked, "Did you ever listen to the Wu Tang Clan?"

It was the first time in hours Nash had spoken. The words felt odd in his mouth.

Pinchot glared up at him with glassy eyes. "What?"

"Wu-Tang Clan. You ever listen to them? You know, 'Protect Ya Neck', 'Bring Da Ruckus', 'Uzi', 'Triumph'? No?" Nash shook his head in mock confusion. "Seriously, 'C.R.E.A.M.' is a stone-cold classic."

Blinking several times, Pinchot's bloody lips quivered. "I... I... No."

"Oh, shame, man, shame. You really should." He inhaled deeply and stretched. "You ever been to the Isle of Capri in Italy?"

"What?" There was genuine confusion on Pinchot's face.

"No, Capri. Anywhere around the Gulf of Naples, really. Stunning part of the world. Have you been?"

"I, yes..."

Nash slapped Pinchot across the face. Not a polite slap,

either. Two of the chair legs lifted into the air, only to be righted when Nash pulled him back.

"Stop." Pinchot whimpered. All vestiges of heroic fortitude finally melted away. The man was beaten. "Stop. Please."

Years of experience kicked in. *Now. Ask him now.*

"Jack, what happened to Tyler Sikes?"

His gaze betrayed him. Normally, the ex-CIA operative would never have given away such an obvious tell. But that was before the hours of torture. Now, his eyes gave it all away. The old cliché said that if someone's eyes darted to the upper right, it signalled deceit. In Nash's experience, that was bullshit. But Pinchot's eyes gazed to the left, then grew wider and darted to the right as if correcting the original thought. That was enough.

Doing his best to right himself, Pinchot asked, "Who?"

"Dude. Really?" Unable to help himself, Nash laughed. "Come on. We both know the man we should have killed but didn't." He took on a more conciliatory tone. "We left him in the desert. Hearn and I went one way and you and Travis went the other." He rocked on his heels. "Except, you didn't, did you?" Leaning down to meet Pinchot's glassy eyes, Nash tilted his head. "I'm guessing you went back for the hacker genius and offered him a job, or at least safe passage for information. Something."

"I don't know what—"

"How is it that the man we left for dead turns up on an assassin's computer at the same time you so miraculously happen to be in the country? I don't think it's being overly paranoid to assume you pulling a gun on me indicated you had something to hide. Now, Jack," Nash took his time to slowly open and close the bloody pliers, "where is Tyler Sikes?"

Pinchot's eyes were focused on the rusty pliers. "That man no longer exists."

"Are you saying he's dead, or he's changed identity?"

Pinchot didn't answer. He appeared to be rallying the last remnants of his reserves to mount a final defence. Nash sighed. There was no use holding out now, it wouldn't stave off the inevitable. No one knew where they were, there would be no last-minute rescue. Still, the man was courageous. He'd fought bravely for hours. Shame it would be to no end.

It still scared Nash how easily he fell back into the deadly skills he'd vowed to never to use again. He wondered what other vows he could break so easily. Stepping towards Pinchot, he opened the pliers.

No matter what Nash did over the next thirty pain-drenched minutes, Pinchot steadfastly refused to tell him what had become of the man who had once been Tyler Sikes.

He did extract something else, however. Delirious from the pain and loss of blood, Pinchot mumbled a single word.

Tartarus.

Not sure what it meant, Nash persisted, but it soon became evident Pinchot had been pushed beyond the point of lucidity. When he wasn't blacked out, he rambled mindlessly, or in short bursts of coherence he venomous vowed gruesome revenge.

At around ten in the morning Nash called it quits. Packing up his gear and cleaning up as best he could, he realised how physically drained he was. He pushed through. He extracted a syringe and administered one final dose for Pinchot.

Minutes later, Nash threw the duffel bag in the back seat of Harry's Charger. Now in broad daylight, he could see the magnificent mansion above the tree line. There were no pangs of familiarity as he gazed at the majestic sandstone edifice.

Amazingly, Pinchot had gotten that part right. The old isolated building that had been his place of torture had had once been part of Nash's family's estate. Built in the 1800s, a teenage Nash had used the isolated shack for far more pleasurable activities with the local ladies. Now the building was the only piece of heritage left in his hands.

Nash realised he needed to go totally dark. He had to disappear from the face of the earth, and soon. At every turn he faced adversaries, even those he'd once considered allies. What he had in mind needed to be done alone, and from the darkest shadows.

Walking around the back of the shack, Nash checked for prying eyes. Beyond a low dilapidated stone wall, he dug into the dirt until he found a heavy chain. Giving it a heave, it took all his reserves of strength to budge the sheet metal cover.

Years before, Nash had buried a couple of old stone watering troughs which had been adjacent to the shack. He'd added to the mounds of dirt surrounding them until the site looked like any other small hill in the neglected part of the old estate.

As the metal cover slid off, a highly illegal collection of heavy armaments and ammunition was revealed. The cache also contained wooden boxes holding silver, gold, passports and IDs. Nash took several pieces from each. He didn't know when he would be back, if ever.

He recovered his stash and returned to the car. Turning the key, the beast roared to life, its rhythmic thrum somehow soothing. As he slowly drove up the gravel road, he saw the back of his family's old mansion looming over the surrounding forest. He wondered if in different circum-stances he'd be struck with a sense of sentimentality. Nash honestly didn't know.

Pinchot was right about one thing. The torture was no good for Nash's karma. He felt sick to his chakras. Nash looked at his hands; they were still shaking. The PTSD dissociation had worn off and he was left with the regret for everything he'd done. This went beyond a slip in judge-ment. It was a full-on leap into a wickedness of the soul he wasn't sure he would ever recover from.

If he ever discovered what Nash had done, his PTSD counsellor would hang up his shingle and find a new profession. Nash was going to have to do a hell of a lot of work to get back to where he'd been, if he ever could. That was a distant piece of personal and spiritual growth he'd have to work on. If he even survived.

But first, he had a very un-zen-like task. Nash didn't know who was behind all this but he was going to find out, and he was going to karma the fuck out of them.

CHAPTER
SEVEN

O nce on the highway and sure he had no tail, Nash used voice commands to make a call and put it on speaker.

The caller answered immediately. "You scratched her, didn't you?"

After the intense last few hours, Nash couldn't help but laugh. "No, not a one. I'll even fill her up before I drop her off."

"You better. You know how much it costs to run a V8 in London?" There was a pause as Harry's voice took on a sombre tone. "Is it done?"

"It is."

"Are you... okay?"

"No." Nash felt his reply answered all possible permutations of the question. "I have a little research task for you."

"I'm all ears and search engines."

"I need you to find anything you can on Tartarus."

It was the single word he'd managed to torture out of Pinchot. If he were honest, his hopes weren't high. The man had been close to delirium, he could have been reciting nursey rhymes for all the sense he was making.

Harry checked the spelling, then asked, "What am I looking for exactly?"

"Anything. To me it sounds like some kind of code word or organisation title. Maybe a front organisation, I really don't know. Anything you can find, really. Besides the historic meaning."

"Historic?"

Behind the wheel, Nash nodded to no one. "Tartarus is from ancient Greece. It was supposedly hidden in the deep abyss of the underworld, used as a dungeon of torment and suffering for the wicked and the wretched. Tartarus was meant to be the place where souls were judged and the wicked received divine punishment."

Harry let out a low whistle. "So I'm looking for someone reaaaally pretentious then?"

Nash chuckled. "Seems that way."

"What next, Nash?"

He had to hand it to Harry, she always cut to the point. "I'm going to sell a kidney to fill up this beast of yours, drop her off unscathed, visit a friend and then disappear off the face of the Earth for a while."

"Visit a friend?"

"Yeah. I owe someone a favour."

THIS WAS the last place Nash had ever thought he'd be again. Certainly not voluntarily. Yet here he was—again. He'd once called the ugly industrial modernist building at Vauxhall Cross home. Now the SIS headquarters made him uneasy, for countless reasons.

It felt strange to walk the halls of his old hunting ground. A few people recognised Nash and greeted him warmly. These people had seemed like family once. Now he felt like an interloper. Like an ex-husband at family reunion.

After Nash turned up unannounced, Paul had extricated himself from a briefing and brought Nash up to his office, with its pleasant view of the Thames. The two exchanged brief small talk before sitting at a small table in the corner of the room.

"You look like shit." Paul handed Nash a cup of tea.

"You really are a smooth talker. You should teach classes." Nash took a sip of tea. "I've had a rough few days."

"I know." Paul as he flicked his hand toward the door of his office. "People out there missed you. You can come back any time, you know that."

Nash amusingly regarded his friend. "You know I'd never come back. Why ask?"

"Being polite."

"That's not the Paul Cavendish I know."

"I'm trying new things. I had a popcorn-flavoured craft beer last week."

"And?"

"Tasted much like you'd expect a cinema manager's arsehole to taste like."

The two exchanged amused looks and sat in comfortable silence for a moment.

"Oh, before I forget, is Atticus Wolfe about?" Nash reached for his wallet. "I owe him a tenner."

"You do like balancing the ledger, don't you?"

"It's a failing of mine, I know."

Paul shifted uncomfortably in his chair. "Atticus is, uh, he's no longer with us."

"Gone private sector, has he?"

"It's... look, Atticus's whereabouts is... complicated." Paul scratched the back of his head. "Really complicated, as it turns out."

"How so?"

Seemingly against his will, Paul let out a huge belly laugh. "The best philosophers in world would struggle with that one."

Knowing he wasn't going to find out the true story of Atticus Wolfe's whereabouts, Nash decided to move on. Paul was one step ahead of him.

"What's this about, Mason?"

"Firstly, I wanted to thank you in person for pulling out all stops with the helicopter thing."

"My pleasure."

"Was it?"

"Not at all."

The men shared a knowing smile.

Nash went on. "Secondly, it's about what we were discussing. Balancing ledgers. I stumbled on some information potentially related to the attacks."

"Stumbled on, eh?" Paul was a smart man; he knew better than to ask what that meant.

"Well, 'information' is a stretch. It's a word, really."

Although Paul was his friend, Nash wasn't about to trust anyone entirely. Especially not now. He needed to gauge Paul's reaction.

He waited a moment, then said, "The word is Tartarus."

There was no reaction. Not even a flicker of recognition.

"Isn't that an old Roman thing?"

"Greek, yes."

"And this word you delivered with such great gravitas, what does it mean?"

Nash ran his fingers through his hair. "I'm not entirely sure, but it's somehow connected to all the people attacking me recently, so I thought I'd share it in case they succeed."

Paul steepled his fingers. "I know I'm going to regret asking this, but how did you come across this information—well, this word?"

From his backpack, Nash pulled out the laptop he'd discovered in the safehouse and placed it on the table. Over the next few minutes, Nash proceeded to tell Paul what he knew, which wasn't a lot. He mentioned Pinchot and the fact that his ex-colleague had pulled a gun on him. He told Paul that he'd obtained the word Tartarus from the man, although he chose not to explain how. The countenance on his old boss's face was enough to tell Nash he'd filled in the gaps himself.

Nash nodded to the laptop. "That's all yours."

Paul tapped it with his index finger. "Maybe the boffins in the lab can crack it."

"They may need to set aside some time." Nash thought back to the conversation he'd had with Harry and smiled. "Apparently six quadrillion years, give or take."

With a quizzical expression, Paul looked out to the Thames for a moment. "What now for you?"

"That's the other reason I came by. I wanted you to know I'm going dark for a bit. Before I did, I wanted to clear the ledger and give you everything I had."

Paul turned and raised an eyebrow. "Clear the ledger?"

"You came to my aid, twice in fact. To make sure I was okay after the first attack, and organising the police when the gunship was up my arse. I don't like debts to go unpaid."

That made Paul smile. "There aren't many in this business with that sense of balance, my friend."

"I'm not in the business." Nash stood to leave. "Not anymore."

~

THE TUBE WAS ODDLY SOOTHING.

Having been tucked up in his rural lifestyle for months, there was something satisfyingly comforting about the drudgery that was the Underground. It had once been a daily ritual. Now it was a quaint luxury. For all its faults, he did miss London.

Watching the blank faces, he revelled in the once familiar. Most had earphones in. All clearly wished they were somewhere else. No one spoke. He did love the unspoken rule that to carry on a conversation on the Tube was tantamount to taking a dump on the floor. This carriage was thankfully quiet.

Minding the gap at Oxford Circus, Nash transferred to the Central Line. Different carriage, different blank faces. Except one.

It had only been a fleeting glance, but Nash caught it. He'd seen that face on the other line, and now the same person had looked in his direction. It wasn't exactly a face one would forget.

Senses on alert, Nash decided to get off at Bank station and see if he was being paranoid.

Waiting until the last possible moment before the door closed, he leapt onto the platform. His dark-haired pursuer was nowhere in sight. *Assumed* pursuer, he corrected himself.

It took a few minutes before he was satisfied he'd been

overly cautious. The next train arrived six minutes later and he got on, still alert but no longer expecting an assassin's bullet. Settling in, he told himself to go back to his casual people watching as the danger had passed. But the hairs on the back of his head prickled again. Years of experience had taught him to trust his instinct.

He stood and roamed the carriage, not entirely sure what he was looking for. Then he found her. Sitting in a baseball cap that she hadn't been wearing before, the athletic young woman appeared to be reading a news article on her phone.

"You've got decent skills, I'll give you that."

The woman didn't even flinch. *She's good.*

"I said, you're good."

The woman turned, giving what in other circumstances would have been a good approximation of surprise. "Are you talking to me?"

The accent was Australian. She had a casual air about her, but instinct told Nash there was danger beneath the tattooed exterior.

"Look, I'm flattered, okay." She smiled sweetly. "You have a nice face, but I'm seeing someone."

She's very good.

Nash leaned against a pole. He suddenly remembered that a while back, Paul had taken on a protégée at MI6 who happened to be Australian. It was something to do with the whole Horatio Lancing affair and its aftermath, although he couldn't recall the details.

"Paul sent you to keep an eye on me, did he?"

"Who?" Although the question was straightforward, it was delivered with enough humour to make it clear she knew she'd been made.

"Is this guy bovering you?"

They turned to see a plump, angry looking chav in a white Lacoste tracksuit, chunky gold necklace and white athletic shoes. He struck Nash as someone who had more trainers than brain cells.

"I'm fine, thank you," the woman answered politely but with enough force to let him know his chivalry was unrequired.

"Move on, grandpa." The chav gave Nash's shoulder a forceful poke with his chubby fingers.

The woman sighed, annoyed. "I don't need saving, okay? I'm not a damsel in distress. This is the London Tube, I'm well adept at fending for myself against creepy men, manspreading and mansplainers. Men, basically."

"So, which one am I?" Nash asked with humour.

The woman gave him an apologetic grin.

"Hey, mate, I'm talkin' to you, a'right?" It seemed the chav was in no mood to take a hint.

Raising her voice, the woman said, "Listen, I'm fine..."

"You deaf, you old geezer?"

It was obvious the chav wasn't concerned with the woman's opinion, more interested in picking a fight with someone he thought was an easy mark. Unfortunately for him, he'd picked the wrong man on the wrong day.

Nash turned slowly to the man. The chav baulked when he saw that Nash displayed none of the fear he'd tried to instil. It seemed the thick-headed thug was realising Nash wasn't the easy target he'd expected.

Nash addressed him, square-jawed. "Listen, it's plain that this lady is in no need of your valiant succour. Grown-ups are talking here. Sod off, you inbred chav. I'm sure there's meth that needs smoking under a bridge somewhere."

The punch was so telegraphed it may as well have come

from Samuel Morse himself. As the chav threw the right cross, Nash shifted his feet ever so slightly and used a feather-light movement of the back of his hand to guide the other man's fist right into the carriage's pole. The resulting scream jarred the entire carriage.

Cradling his mangled hand, the chav screamed, "You broke my fuckin' fist, you did!"

"I think you'll find you did that all yourself, my friend."

Pulling back his uninjured left fist, the chav readied himself for another round, though far less self-assured than the first. As he was about to attempt another blow, the dark-haired woman stood and intercepted the punch herself. Using a defensive move Nash could have sworn was a Krav Maga, she deflected the strike while simultaneously taking out his knees. The end result was a crumbled chav, his face landing inelegantly on an unattended plastic seat.

In an unsteady stupor from the blows, and with a nose gushing blood, the chav stood, seething. As he staggered forward, the tattooed woman grabbed the back of his head and spun it with surprising speed, using his momentum and adding some her own until both his arms were pinned behind his back and his face was pressed against the door.

The woman has moves.

As if on cue, the train arrived at the next station and she pushed him out onto the platform. Having finally learned his lesson, the chav stood there, dumbfounded, and gave a slight whimper for effect. The man's white designer tracksuit was streaked with his own blood.

Nash tilted his head. "You should get that seen to mate, just to be on the safe side."

In a daze, the chav nodded. He seemed unsure how he'd ended up where he stood.

As the doors began to close, the woman raised her voice

in his direction. "And you should think about your fucken' life choices, mate."

The door closed and the train moved on, leaving the bewildered chav to do exactly that.

Glancing around the carriage, Nash saw that every eye was on them. Addressing the woman, he said in a low voice, "Given the audience, should we..." Nash motioned to the next carriage.

The raven-haired woman gestured for Nash to lead the way. They moved through the doors connecting the carriages and soon found a pair of unoccupied seats.

The woman shook her head. "That crack about meth needing smoking under a bridge somewhere. That's gold."

"What's your name?"

She told him. He didn't believe her.

"I'm going to have to get you to repeat that." For a moment Nash thought his hearing was going. It wasn't every day you met someone with such a unique name.

The pretty woman sighed as if she'd heard it a million times. "It's my real name. Promise."

Nash had no choice but to believe her. Why would someone pretend to have such an absurd name? Nash had to accept he'd just met someone called Eva Destruction.

He was right. His old boss had sent someone to help, whether he wanted it or not. He didn't.

Moving on from the name, with some effort, Nash said, "I appreciate Paul's help, but the whole lone wolf slipping into the shadows thing is difficult when someone else comes along for the ride."

Eva tapped her foot. "I've heard your name spoken a lot."

Tilting his head, Nash said, "There are so many ways to take that statement, I don't know where to begin."

"Paul holds you in high regard, and that's no small praise." She smiled. It was a genuine, wide smile. There was no denying the woman was stunning. "You can't go this alone, Nash. You need my help."

"I need your help, or Paul wants to keep an eye on me?"

"You're welcome to choose one." She issued a blank stare. "Going alone hasn't exactly worked out for you of late. You need a partner to watch your back. What do you say?"

A middle-aged, conservatively dressed woman turned to them and issued a stern, "Shhh."

Eva's head darted around and, nice as pie, she said, "Shush, yourself, you fuckmuppet. We're having a polite conversation so you can bippity boppety back the fuck up, you posh twat." She waved her hand dismissively and turned away. "Fuckety bye."

The woman's mouth dropped open and those without headphones did their best not to laugh out loud. Eva turned back to Nash, serene as could be.

"Where were we?"

Nash frowned. "This is your idea of stealth, is it?"

Without taking her eyes off him, Eva asked quietly, "Is anyone looking at us or have they all turned away?"

Nash glanced around. Not a single person in the carriage looked their way. *Unorthodox, but effective.*

"Huh." He did his best to remain on topic. "Uh, you were asking if you could be my partner and I was wondering if I had a choice."

She patted Nash's arm. "I'm reminded of an old Australian band called Mental As Anything, who had a hit with 'If You Leave Me Can I Come Too?'."

"There is no way anything in that sentence is remotely true."

Eva sat with her arms crossed and an air of quiet determination. She didn't strike Nash as someone easily dissuaded.

It seemed Nash had a partner, whether he liked it or not. And a sweary one at that.

EIGHT

"I work—"

"Alone," Eva finished Nash's sentence as they exited Hackney Wick station. "Yes, so you said." She strode with purpose, as if she was aware of their destination. For all he knew, she was. "But the way I see it, whoever is after you has a fuck-ton of money and resources. Assassins aren't cheap. Gunships aren't cheap. In the movies the lone white man is cool and resourceful and always saves the day, but in reality, he's going to end up deader than a naked pacifist in no-man's land."

"That's a hell of an analogy." Nash scratched the back of his neck. "You have a way with words."

"Fucken' A, I do."

Reaching Wallace Road, he pointed towards their destination. Eva proceeded without question.

There were a very small number of people Nash trusted. Paul Cavendish was one of the select few. If Paul trusted this woman enough for him to send her to protect Nash, he would return the favour and trust her in return. Until there was evidence to do otherwise, that was. Trust only went so far.

Nash was still coming to grips with the concept of having a partner. Yes, on missions he'd usually been teamed with others—although not always—but he'd been out of the game so long it took some getting used to. In fact, he wasn't entirely sure what mission he was on. Sure, he had people trying to kill him, but... He didn't finish the thought. There was no need. If Eva were to put her eloquence to it, she would tell him he was absolutely on a mission and he needed to get on with it and shut the fuck up. He really hoped her potty mouth didn't rub off on him.

"Why are you here, Nash?" Eva walked on, keeping her gaze forward.

"Uh, you're the one following me."

"No, I mean, why are you actively pursuing whoever is behind this?"

"You expect me to simply let it go?"

Eva squinted. "So this is about revenge, then?"

"No, I just want to know who's trying to kill me. I think that's fair and reasonable."

She remained calm. "So you can kill them?"

"No. I don't do that."

Folding her arms, Eva said, "I heard different. I've read some of your mission reports. There's red all over them. You were a machine."

Nash glared. "I don't do that *anymore*."

"Why, because you retired?"

Nash felt he was being baited, but went on regardless. "No, because I'm a pacifist."

"Just curious, do pacifists usually kill three assassins before dinner?"

"I didn't mean to."

Finally Eva turned to him. "That either makes you incompetent or a liar."

"I, look..."

She cut in. "Or torture a poor man to death."

The pang of regret stabbed Nash like a million red hot pokers. "Poor man? He tried to kill me."

"For a pacifist, you sure have a lot of people trying to kill you."

"To be honest, I wish they weren't."

"Do you?" Eva stopped walking, forcing Nash to do the same.

"Do I what?"

"Do you really wish you weren't mixed up in all this?"

"I just said I did."

"Yeah," Eva tilted her head, and her delivery grew more animated, like she'd finally got to her point, "and I asked if you were bullshitting. I heard you were a school teacher. That's a noble profession, but dude, after the life you lived is it really fulfilling? I tried to go back to being a barista after I got involved in all this but in all honesty, reality no longer cut it. It's like if the blokes who walked on the moon then tried to work as a shoe salesman or something. Once you hit those highs, civilian life just doesn't keep the loins moist, you know?"

"I'm not sure I do."

"Yeah, you do. I saw your eyes with the dude on the Tube. I doubt those peepers ever spark like that when you're grading papers or telling Mrs Johnson little Timmy could really do well if he just applied himself and stopped furiously masturbating at the back of maths class."

"History."

"What's that?"

"I teach history, not maths."

Eva tilted her head. "And is there a Timmy who furiously masturbates at the back of class?"

"No." Nash paused. "His name is Nathan."

Eva laughed, breaking the tension. "I think you really need to determine why you're here. Is it really because you want to find out who's behind this, when there's a multitude of other organisations, *legally* appointed organisations, already on it? Or is it that you miss the life and want back in? You need to gaze a bit inward, my friend."

That was exactly what Nash had been trying to avoid. He'd been actively focused on the mechanics of the investigation and doing everything he could to avoid the emotions of it. He'd known Eva for mere minutes, and already she gave the impression she was more aware of his own feelings than he was. They continued walking without a word.

A few minutes later, Nash and Eva stood before the steel door he'd exited through only hours before, after dropping off Harry's car. He pressed the button on her intercom and waited. Seconds later, Harry appeared on the screen, seemingly annoyed.

"You changed the equaliser settings in my car."

Nash smirked. "The bass was too high."

Beside him, Eva tutted. "Dude, not cool."

"What?" Nash shrugged.

"You never mess with a lady's stereo settings." There was a pause as Harry's eyes shifted to his companion. "Who's the chick?"

"Can we come in?"

"Answer my question first," Harry growled, "then I'll consider yours."

"My name is Eva." She turned to Nash, amused. "I'm his colleague."

Harry's face crumpled into a scowl. "Nash works alone."

Throwing his hands in the air, he replied, "That's what I keep telling everyone."

The door buzzed open and the two entered Harry's expensive apartment. After the briefest of introductions and the offer and refusal of refreshments, Harry's hands went straight to her hips. She jutted her head in Eva's direction, her demeanour sour.

"The image search I ran said your name was Candy Stripe, and that you'd authored several articles in *Rolling Stone* magazine."

Eva grinned sheepishly. "Ah, I can explain..."

"My diagnostic search analysis also determined that the existence of Candy Stripe was bullshit. Totally fake." Harry tapped her foot. "Care to explain that one, *Eva*?"

"Previous mission. Seems they haven't scrubbed it." Eva frowned, impressed. "Jesus on a pogo stick, the best people in the business set that profile up, but you blew it out of the water in seconds. That's pretty impressive."

Harry dodged the compliment. "Mission? You a spook too?"

Eva turned to Nash inquisitively.

He shrugged. "Harry knows everything."

"Everything?"

"Everything." Harry nodded curtly. "I can tell you his first shag was in the back room of a shitty Irish pub. He never married but has had two women propose to him. He had the highest kill ratio while at MI6. He's literally slept with royalty. He once got in a punch on with Elon Musk. And he's got a scar on his left ball after a school mate attacked him with a cricket stump."

Eva turned to Nash and he held up a defensive hand. "Only one of those things isn't true."

The answer seemed to amuse Eva. She turned to Harry. "Yes, I'm a spook."

Harry accepted the reply with a sigh and motioned for them to come in. She offered refreshments once more, and again the offer was politely declined.

Motioning between the two, Eva asked, "Are you two—?"

"Strictly professional," he cut in. Nash realised he'd replied rather quickly.

Eva rolled her eyes. "I wasn't going to ask if you were an item, dude. Settle. It's the twenty-first century. Men and women can work together, grandpa. I was going to ask if you'd been working together long."

Nash growled. "Steady on with the grandpa, thanks."

"Fax machines were the new and exciting thing when you started out, weren't they?"

Harry snickered but didn't interrupt, seemingly amused by the exchange.

"I'm only fifty-five, I'm not old." He paused. "And yes, they were."

Both women laughed, but Nash didn't think they were laughing *with* him. He sighed. "Yes, I'm old and decrepit and know how to use a pencil to fix an MC Hammer cassette when it gets eaten up by the tape player. Now, can we please talk about what we came here for?"

"Of course." Eva bowed her head solemnly. "Just a few quick questions. Did you write on slate at school? Were you friends with the Wright brothers?"

"Yes, very good." Nash rolled his eyes.

Eva regarded him smugly. "When you started in the service did they have flintlock pistols or did you just throw rocks at the Prussians?"

Harry laughed, then waved an apologetic hand in Nash's direction.

Hefting an eyebrow, Nash said, "I forgot to ask, where-abouts in New Zealand are you from?"

Opening her mouth to speak, Eva stopped. "I thought we were being good-natured. That was just low, man. I'm Australian."

"Oh, so both your parents are convicts then?"

Eva tutted. "For a man who's been shot at twice this week, sounds like you're looking for a third."

Chuckling, Harry showed the two to her vintage dining table. Addressing Nash, she flicked a thumb in Eva's direction. "I like her."

Nash's eyes narrowed. "I'm so pleased for you." He sighed. "Maybe I'll have that drink after all. Black coffee for me and a jar of Vegemite for my companion here."

"Funny." Eva turned to Harry and addressed her like an old friend. "I'll have a coffee too, please. Can I help? In my past life I was a barista."

Waving her off, Harry went to the kitchen. "That's good to know, but I've got this."

While Harry made the coffee under Eva's vigilant gaze, Nash brought Harry up to speed, and explained that Paul had thrust Eva into his sphere whether he liked it or not. Nash was pretty sure it was the latter. All the while, Eva watched Harry's coffee making intently, with the occasional wince.

They all sat with piping hot coffees. Eva took hers with thanks, but chose not to comment on the quality.

"So," Harry started, "you need to find a bloke who chooses not to be found." She paused. "I assume you're not going to kill him?"

Nash tilted his head towards her. "Correct."

By way of explanation, Harry faced Eva and nodded towards Nash. "He's gone all zen, you see. Doesn't believe in violence. The only thing he murders now is the occasional curry."

Eva hefted a non-believing eyebrow. "So I've heard."

"I could do with a curry, actually." Nash rubbed his stomach, realising how famished he was.

"I've been looking for your bloke," Harry went on. "It seems Tyler Sikes has been scrubbed from existence, at least as far as the internet is concerned. There's even less on your Tartarus organisation—in fact, there's nothing. It's almost like they don't want to be found."

"Not many secret organisations do."

Eva added, "MI6 have nothing on Sikes since your mission in Al Hudaydah. Even before that, it seems the only info comes from our locally saved sources. He's done a good job convincing the world he never existed."

Harry steepled her fingers and gave a sage bow of her head. "That's because Tyler Sikes no longer exists."

"Cool. Good chat." Nash clapped his hands together. "This is nothing we didn't already know. He's somehow infiltrated every website that ever acknowledged his existence and scrubbed it clean to the bone."

Harry tapped her fingers, deep in thought. "It would take a herculean effort by some brilliant and amazingly talented individual to find even a trace of this guy, I assume." She took a sip of her coffee and raised her eyebrows at him. "I mean, they'd have to be some sort of next-level genius capable of..."

"Alright Einstein, you're incredible and brilliant. Now spill."

Harry beamed. "I may have come up with something..."

"You don't say?"

She winked. "I used next generation facial recognition software to trawl through every picture on the internet—and I mean every. Social media, legit media, so-called private image depositories, the lot."

Eva crinkled her forehead. "MI6 tried that too, we didn't get anywhere."

Nodding in response, Harry replied, "I bet they didn't take into account possible cosmetic procedures. Check it."

Opening her laptop, Harry explained a whole lot of computer programs that went over Nash's head. Eva appeared to follow along fine, and asked some technical questions that seemed to impress Harry. Nash, on the other hand, felt like a five-year-old standing around in a shopping centre while his mum chatted to a friend. He was just waiting for it to end.

"So," Eva leaned forward, far more engrossed than Nash, "your AI program extrapolated likely cosmetic procedures?"

Harry tilted her head. "To an extent. I programmed it based on statistically plausible techniques given an unlimited budget, which I suspect this guy has. It didn't search for every possible permutation, only those likely at the high end of the market."

"So not what he'd look like as a Klingon, then?"

Harry snickered. "Better than a Ferengi."

Both women laughed.

"Are you both still speaking English?" Nash waved at the laptop. "What did you find?"

"Here."

Harry pointed to a news article, written in Portuguese. Four men in suits on a waterfront smiled widely for the camera. There was a vague familiarity about the man on the far left. It was the eyes. His body was positioned in a way that suggested he was surprised to be in the picture. The other three were posed, but he appeared to have been photographed by accident as he passed by.

Nash spoke some Spanish, so was able to get the gist of the first few paragraphs. The businessmen had funded an expansion of the existing marina and this was the grand opening. The caption below the picture claimed the man was Leonard Pace.

Frowning, Nash asked, "This is Sikes?"

"With an eighty-seven per cent probability." Harry chuckled, knowing how lost Nash was. "It *is* Sikes. He's resurfaced under a different persona. Canadian now, apparently. He's now known as Leonard Pace."

Leaning in, Nash examined the face. The cheekbones and the jaw were different, stronger, but the eyes held a distinct air of condescension which was all too familiar. It *could* be him.

Eva scoffed. "This guy's a douchepoodle."

"How do you know that?"

"Out of all the names he could choose, the multitude of names the world has to offer, he went with Leonard?" She shook her head and pointed to the laptop. "Douchepoodle."

Sikes/Pace now hailed from Toronto, although the further Harry searched, the sketchier Leonard Pace's history became. His manufactured persona claimed he was a wealthy investment banker.

"I've never known what that means," Nash said truthfully.

"Me either, all I know is they're rubbish tippers." Eva threw up a frustrated hand. "In my experience, investment bankers are generally wankers."

Harry held up a finger. "Except he's not. Well, not a

banker, I can't speak for the wanker part. Pace's entire history is colostomy bag of lies."

Eva laughed, and nodded in Harry's direction. "I like her."

Harry took the compliment in her stride. "Like our friend Candy Stripe here, his whole persona is bullshit. Articles supposedly years old were only posted in the last nine months or so. Schools where he claimed to be a student have him listed as attending, yet there are no class photos of him, and no school publications of the time ever mention him. In short, super sketchy. As far as I can make out, he's currently living in São Paulo."

Stretching, Eva asked, "I guess we're off to Brazil then?"

Instead of reacting immediately, Nash lost himself in thought. He recalled the near-genius status Sikes held, all his degrees and wunderkind status. The man was a master-mind who had gone to immense effort to disappear off the face of the earth. Or at least, to make it seem that way.

Clicking her fingers in front of his face, Eva interrupted his train of thought. "Hello, Mr Nash, you still with us?"

"I was thinking this seems all too convenient."

"Convenient?" Harry scoffed. "Do you know how many hours I've spent on this shit? I'm the best there is and it took me forever to even find this much." She held both hands out to Eva. "Even MI6 came up with fuck all."

Eva gave Harry finger guns. "Thanks."

"You're welcome."

Nash scratched the back of his neck. "I get that, but this all seems," he waved his hands around vaguely, "too easy. It smells like a trap."

"What exactly does a trap smell like?" Harry asked with a squint.

"Chloroform, talcum powder and Crème de menthe."

Eva raised an eyebrow. "That's weirdly specific."

Nash huffed. "I'm not saying you haven't done great work, Harry, you're awesome. But doesn't all this seem a bit... off?"

Harry eyed her laptop, as if Nash had taken a personal swipe. "You think this is an ambush of some kind?"

Rubbing his chin, Nash contemplated the question. "Maybe."

Eva tilted her head. "So what do we do?"

Nash grinned. "We go to São Paulo."

NINE

"Just a little one."

Eva huffed. "No."

"Even a .22 would be fine," Nash offered thoughtfully.

"No."

"A pointy stick? I can settle for a blunt one, I'll sharpen it myself."

Standing with arms folded in the baggage claim of Guarulhos International Airport, Eva scowled. "You're not getting a weapon. You're not a..." she eyed the other passengers milling about, waiting for their luggage, "member of my organisation. You're not even officially here."

The two had caught the red-eye out of London and slept most of the way. The rest of the time had been made up of small talk and working out how to track down Leonard Pace and determine if he really was Tyler Sikes. There had been little discussion about what would happen if it was. Nash assumed that would come later.

"But I *am* here." Nash poked Eva in the shoulder to

emphasise the point. "If we get into a firefight, I don't think semantics is going to help a hell of a lot. If you could see your way to—"

Eva threw her arms in the air and turned to Nash, incensed. "I'm not fucking getting you a—"

"Hey." He touched Eva's forearm to calm her. "It's okay, I was only asking."

Inhaling deeply, Eva held up a palm in apology. "Sorry... sorry. I'd be asking for the same if the roles were reversed. I'm just a bit..." She jiggled her shoulders.

Saying nothing, Nash waited. Sometimes you gained more from a conversation by allowing the other person to fill the gaps. It often garnered more information than direct questions.

"It's just, I should be in the Maldives right now." Eva let out a big sigh. "I've recently started a new relationship and was looking forward to exploring it, you know? But you understand as well as I do, Paul has this way of asking for things—"

"That seem completely reasonable, so it's not until later you ask what the hell did I just agree to?"

Eva chuckled and regarded the luggage carousel for a time. "Yeah, he really does."

"New relationship? Maldives is a great place for that kind of exploring." He gentled his tone to be more sympathetic. As much as they had politely butted heads, Nash really liked this young woman. She struck him as an extremely bright and competent agent. "Sorry for taking you away from that. None of this was intentional. Here's hoping it's all a wild goose chase and you're on a beach drinking pina coladas before you know it."

"Great." Eva growled. "Now I have that fucking song in my head." She smiled to let him know they were fine, and rocked back and forth on her heels, humming the *Pina Colada Song*.

The luggage carousel wasn't moving and people were everywhere, waiting. It was the real truth about airports; everyone rushes to wait. So they waited.

"Why are you a pacifist?"

Nash turned to Eva, amusement dancing on his face. "You waited the entire flight and you ask me this now?"

"It just struck me, the contradiction of you asking for a..." her eyes checked for any eavesdroppers, "... gun. You won't use it to kill someone, not even in self-defence, so I have to ask why?"

"I'm retired."

"Yes, but that doesn't answer *why*? What made you into this non-lethal super chill dude who walked away from the life? Plenty from our profession retire without feeling the need to become zen masters. Some become gardeners. Others consultants. One, I heard, even went into painting teeny tiny Warhammer models. But you're the first I've ever heard of who turned his back on the very thing that made him such a formidable adversary."

Nash tilted his head to acknowledge the point. For Eva, violence was a necessity, however loathsome or distasteful it may be. She served King and Country, and it was an unfortunate truth that bloodshed came with the territory. For someone who still lived in that world, his views were as antithetical as a vegan butcher or a parking officer with a heart.

"I was good at it. The killing, I mean." Nash hoped he sounded as at ease as he felt. There was no malice in her queries. "I was very, very good. But I began to question whether I wasn't part of the problem. Violence begetting violence and all that. What if we all just stopped? War and death bring nothing but suffering, economic damage and, more than anything, moral and spiritual degradation. It never stops. One group will vow revenge and it perpetuates itself, forever. Literally, forever. All of recorded history tells us it keeps going—and I should know, I teach history now. So, one day I asked myself what if we collectively said, you know what? I'm not doing it anymore. Fuck it, I'm going to *not* be the problem."

"Grand idea until someone points a gun in your face."

"So I've discovered." Nash sighed. "I vowed after my last mission that there would be no more. I can't control the rest of the world, but if I do what I can, what's right, maybe others can too."

Images of Al Hudaydah and the sniper's scope vision of Qasim's head exploding came rushing back. It was a final, bloody, full stop to his former life.

Or so he'd hoped.

His thoughts turned towards more recent acts and he sighed more heavily than he'd intended. "Unfortunately, people keep trying to kill me. They've dragged back into this world." He rubbed the back of his neck. "Once we've found Sikes, I'll get back to it and try to atone for all the evil I've wreaked."

They fell into an uncomfortable silence, Eva swapping glances between her phone and the non-moving baggage carousel. From the fervour with which she typed, he assumed she was messaging the companion she was no longer going to meet in the Maldives.

While they waited, Nash did what he normally did in any densely populated area: he observed the crowd, searching for potential threats. It was never the muscled long-haired biker types like in the movies. The biggest threats always came from those you least suspected. In espionage, a good spy blended into the background like wallpaper. It took a keen eye to spot real danger. Unless they were extremely good, it was always the eyes that gave them away. Especially in places like airports, where most people kept to themselves, doing their best to avoid inter-actions with the rest of humanity. Most had their eyes glazed over with the tedium of flying. Nash gravitated towards anyone displaying a modicum of alertness.

He found one. Watching from the corner of his eye, he observed the target, using long-dormant skills. He leaned towards Eva, his gaze on the crowd, his voice low.

"What are three words guaranteed to liven up any conversation?"

"I am bi. No, wait, I've a sex swing. Is sex swing two words?"

Nash crossed his arms. "I don't think—"

"I know, I know!" She pointed with confidence. "I bought lube."

He turned to her. "Are all your observations sexual?"

Eva shrugged. "Mostly."

"Do you take anything seriously?"

"Scrabble." Eva huffed. "Can't stand it when people try to use abbreviations or anything with an apostrophe. It's in the rules, always has been, but no, people keep trying." She paused, realising Nash was annoyed. "So, what three words were you thinking?"

"We've got company."

"Oh, yeah, that's a good one." Her face turned sombre. "Wait, you're serious?"

It was miraculous how quickly the woman put on her game face. He even noticed the subtle shifting of her feet into a fighting stance. She followed Nash's gaze to a tall, dark-skinned woman in a business suit standing to their left. Her hair was so short she was practically bald. She attempted to appear casual, but her alert eyes deliberately slid around Eva and Nash. She was trying incredibly hard not to gaze in their direction. When the woman's gaze returned to the baggage belt, Eva gave him the slightest of nods. Suddenly the two were partners, working in unison.

Eva's outward appearance was as friendly as ever, but her tone carried far more weight than it had only moments before. "I'll make like I'm getting my luggage then pretend it's not mine. I'll make my way to the left so she's between us."

Nash grunted his approval. Eva set off on her journey of deception. He could have put his observation down to paranoia, but the fact that Eva had so suddenly validated his instincts felt good. Was he actually pleased he'd identified a threat?

Before he had a chance to unpack that realisation, the woman walked directly towards Nash. She stopped before him, unsmiling, all business.

"You are Mister Nash?" Her striking features and glowing skin made her look more like a supermodel than a businesswoman.

"I'm terribly sorry, I think you have me mistaken for someone else." Nash was reasonably proud of his approximation of an Australian accent.

The woman waited for Eva to make her way back and then gave her a curt bow. "Agent Destruction, my name is Hadiza Nnadi."

"Ah, agent Nnadi, pleased to meet you." She turned to Nash. "She's our local contact here." Turning back to the woman, she said, "I thought we were meeting at the field office tomorrow?"

"There was a change of plans." Nnadi turned to Nash. "Your South African accent is appalling."

He grimaced. "I was trying for Australian."

"Oh, dude." Eva scowled. "Don't do that."

Thankfully Nash spotted both their suitcases and excused himself. When he returned, Nnadi ushered them through customs without the usual checks and they walked towards her Volkswagen.

As he followed the two young women, all Nash could think was, *Why does it seem everyone who works for MI6 these days is about twelve years old?*

"Mr Pace has the penthouse in the new marina apartment complex. He's been living there for eight months," Nnadi said as she drove down the Rodovia dos Imigrantes, or Immigrants Highway, the main road to the port town of Santos.

"Does he do much business here in Brazil?"

Nnadi replied, "His tax return last year stated he made about the right amount of money to live in the penthouse. His source of income was listed as investment banker. We don't have much more detail than that."

In the back seat, Eva and Nash exchanged glances. The closer they got to the target, the more sceptical Nash became. It wasn't just the convenient—no matter how much Harry protested—uncovering of Sikes' potential alias, there was more to it. If all trace of Sikes had been wiped off the planet five years ago, then how could his name appear on a laptop hidden in a safehouse?

Were all these clues laid out for Nash to find in some elaborate and unknown scheme, or was it that they were simply damn good spies? Or was it all a useless wild goose chase? He had no way of telling. But Nash had survived long enough to retire from espionage by trusting his instinct, and his gut told him something was off. If only his gut was a little more specific. Regardless, their operation was on less assured footing with each passing minute.

"Where exactly are you taking us?" Nash hoped his voice didn't carry the doubt he felt.

"I thought you'd want to scope the penthouse from a distance first—I assumed you'd want to get straight into it. I've booked a table at a restaurant across the water with a good view of it. I thought we could eat and discuss next steps. I have a plan I'd like to discuss with you both. Plus, they do a kick-arse paella."

The fact Nnadi had already picked a restaurant over-looking their target, an hour's drive away from São Paulo struck Nash as odd. Then again, he could be overthinking everything. He turned to Eva to see if she had caught any of Nash's doubts, but she was sitting passively, apparently indifferent to Nnadi's dinner reservations.

Nash wished he could punch his guts to either stop casting doubts over everything or provide some concrete answers. His gut remained mute on the matter. That was, until he thought of paella and his stomach grumbled. Not exactly what he had in mind.

"How long have you been with MI6, Agent Nnadi?" Eva asked.

"Oh, coming up to five years now. A field agent for three. All those spent in South America. The last two I've been stationed here."

"You like it?" Again, Nash hoped his tone was friendly.

"Oh, for sure. The current government keeps us busy. If it's not an impeachment, it's some other scandal. Our field office is pretty solid, can't complain. I'm due to rotate out at the end of the year. I'm hoping Washington, but so is every other mug on the continent, so who knows?"

At the mention of MI6 politics, Nash once again wondered how he'd become embroiled in it all over again. He'd left the organisation because he'd grown disillusioned with what they'd become—bloated, overly-bureaucratic, and heavy reliant on passive data mining rather than real field work. His nascent pacifist beliefs had only grown stronger the further he'd gone from the Secret Intelligence Service.

Just how, then, had he arrived here? He'd made it out. All the way out. He was a school teacher, living a boring life in a sleepy town where the highlight of his week should have been flirting with a waitress. Now he was in Brazil on a mission suitable for someone half his age. He *was* on a mission with people half his age. He shook his head.

"Something wrong?"

Nash wasn't sure if the concern on Eva's face was reflective of his own or completely of her own making. "Sorry, I was stumbling down a line of thinking that's not entirely helpful." He cracked his neck in a way his mother always hated. "All good," he lied, "just eager to get stuck in."

And get stuck in they did. The three had a pleasant dinner across from potential-Pace/Sikes' apartment. It was unfortunate that their vantage point failed to afford them a view in; the angle was too steep. Nnadi was right about one thing, though. The paella was kick-arse.

Scraping his plate clean, Nash said, "You mentioned you had a plan?"

Nnadi smiled. "See the luxury yacht over there?"

"The one as big as the horizon? It's hard to miss."

Eva was right. The yacht was massive. To call it a yacht

was underselling it. Superyacht came closer, but still didn't completely hit the mark. Megayacht was most accurate; the craft had multiple decks and opulence dripping from every fitting. To Nash, it was the kind of vessel movie stars or drug dealers hosted birthdays on for their much younger boyfriends or girlfriends. It was not a yacht of subtlety.

"Tomorrow night there's going to be a Brazil Independence Day party on that yacht, the *Nao To Nem Ai*."

Nash squinted as he did the translation. "I don't even care?"

In response, Nnadi gave a slight shake of her head. "That's the informal translation. There's a more formal meaning."

Eva and Nash exchanged glances once more.

Nnadi went on. "The party will be hosted by none other than Mr Leonard Pace."

"He chartered the yacht?" Nash asked.

"He *owns* the yacht." Nnadi shifted in her chair, seemingly glad she had their rapt attention. "I used one of my contacts at the *Folha de S.Paulo* newspaper to wrangle us an invite. There will be about a hundred and fifty guests, so we should be able to blend in."

"A yacht?" Nash scratched his significant beard. "It doesn't exactly give us a lot of escape options should something go wrong."

"I've thought of that." Eva tapped the table. "I have some ideas."

She briefly contemplated the megayacht. Nash could almost hear the gears turning. Nnadi opened her leather folder and held aloft three elegant, gilded envelopes.

She handed the first invitation to Eva. "You're Penelope Knightsbridge."

Swivelling her head from side to side, Eva said, "I'm so fucken posh."

The second, she handed to Nash. "You're Douglas Maloney."

Nash groaned. "Do I seriously look like a Douglas?"

Both women replied, deadpan, "Yes."

Ignoring the apparent insult, Nash asked, "Is this thing formal?"

Nnadi raised an eyebrow. "Very."

"We're going to need some clothes. Fancy ones at that."

Nnadi waggled her eyebrows and gave a smug grin. "A tailor will visit your hotel room at nine tomorrow and have your suit ready by two o'clock." She turned to Eva. "A stylist will meet you in the lobby at ten. They will take you to several boutique designers to source you an evening gown."

"Excellent work." Nash winced. "I'm sorry, I didn't mean that condescendingly. I don't want to sound like I'm mansplaining or whatever it is. I just meant it was good work, genuinely."

Both women traded amused smirks. Eva spoke first.

"You're allowed to compliment, dude. That's fine. It's when a man adds a 'for a girl' at the end of the sentence he's asking for a genital punch. You're golden."

They ordered another round of caipirinhas and planned the following evening. The more they spoke, the more Nash stamped down his earlier wariness. The process of planning a mission reinvigorated him. It felt natural. It felt like home. Perhaps he was where he needed to be.

He also felt a renewed sense of optimism that they weren't on a wild goose chase. The name of the yacht, *Nao To Nem Ai*, formally translated to "I'm not even here".

Perhaps they had found the elusive Sikes after all.

CHAPTER
TEN

"Comms test. Repeat, comms test. Acknowledge. Over."

Nash walked slowly towards the hulking megayacht in his custom-made, fitted tuxedo. His earpiece was flesh-coloured and invisible, unless someone looked close enough. The hidden lapel mic was top of the range.

So far, Nnadi had displayed excellent planning skills. The tailor had shown up at exactly nine and had supplied him with a superb Tom Ford tuxedo. A hairdresser turned up soon after and gave him what Eva later assured him was a "sweet-arse fuckboy haircut". The hairdresser also trans-formed his unkept beard into a stylish Van Dyke style, which he had to admit suited him. From the outside, at least, he gave the impression of someone who was part of the diamond-dripped set. The crowd was just as formal as he was.

He had to admit, the new haircut and styled beard had shaved years off his appearance. He almost felt it. Then again, it might be the fact he was on a mission once more. It was an aspect of his life he'd stopped longing for years ago but it seemed it hadn't stopped longing for him.

"Hear you loud and clear," Eva replied. He hadn't seen her yet, but Nash knew she was somewhere milling about in the growing crowd. "Also, your arse looks great in that tux."

Nash sighed. "Can we have a bit more formality in the protocols, please? Over."

"Anything you say. Sierra, marzipan, Zulu, fisting, chlamydia, over."

Nnadi laughed. "I can hear you both clearly." There was a pause. "By the way, the beard suits you. Gives you a sexy silver fox vibe. You're so going to score tonight."

Groaning, Nash replied, "I'm not here to—"

"We're just joking dude, chill." Eva's voice turned business-like. "We all know exactly why we're here."

Both women had spotted him, but he hadn't seen them among the crowd of black tuxedos and elegant dresses. There was a fair complement of black-clad security guards, too. Though they smiled genially and guided the guests cordially towards the yacht, their neck tattoos, facial scars, military haircuts and sidearms gave Nash a different impression altogether. The high rollers probably got a kick out of being in the presence of such dangerous ruggedness; at arm's length, of course.

Taking his eyes off security, Nash casually scanned the crowd and his jaw dropped. About twenty metres behind him, Eva glowed in an ethereal light. She attracted the gaze of all in her orbit, men and women alike, in her jade-green silk backless dress, which clung to her every curve. Even with the multitude of tattoos—or perhaps because of them—her stunning beauty shone through. The chunky bracelet on her arm added a touch of elegance, if there was room for more. She seemed utterly unaware of her exquisiteness, which only added to her allure. She glided across the pier as if she'd been to a million super-rich events. Perhaps she had.

The thought triggered a memory in the back of Nash's mind. There was some connection between Eva and the disappearance of Horatio Lancing, who had once been the richest man in the world. For the life of him he couldn't recall what it was. The distracting thought was soon dismissed as she sashayed up to Nash. There was no denying the woman had an air of sophisticated elegance about her.

She hooked her arm through Nash's and beamed. "This G-string is right up my clacker."

Trying his best not to choke, he replied, "Look, I don't officially know what a clacker is, but I have my suspicions. Let's keep the mystery alive, shall we?"

"Looking schmick, old man."

Judging by her delivery, Nash assumed schmick was a positive Australian word of some description. It appeared Eva was determined to keep up with her playful "old man" digs. Nash had to admit they were nowhere near as grating as they had once been.

"Now Eva," Nnadi said through the earpiece, "didn't anyone teach you to respect your elders?"

"You two are hysterical." Nash tried in vain to hide his amusement.

"Hey Nnadi, we should be thankful Nash is with us. It's six o'clock, well past his dinner time. He's a little a trooper. If he keeps this up he could even stay up until, I don't know, nine, maybe even nine thirty."

Nash rolled his eyes and nodded towards Eva's arm,

which was intertwined with his. "I thought we were all entering the party separately?"

Eva wrinkled her nose. "Nnadi and I discussed it on the way here, it makes sense for you to board the yacht with one of us. You're the indestructible lone wolf mister solo guy, remember? If this really is Sikes' ship then his people might be on the lookout for someone who meets that criteria. You'll be less conspicuous with a lady on your arm, don't you think?"

Nash had no doubt he'd be less noticeable with Eva by his side. One's gaze naturally gravitated in her direction. He could have been invite-less and naked and no one would even peek in his direction.

"Speaking of ladies..." Eva pointed towards the right, where several well-dressed guests awaited their turn to ascend the gangway.

Nnadi was giving Eva a run for her money. In a strapless orange satin gown, Nnadi glowed. If Eva was stunning, Nnadi was striking. Her strong features were complemented by her bright yet soft dress. She could have just stepped off a Milan runway.

Despite his earlier self-confidence, Nash was increasingly feeling like the thorn between roses. Pushing down his misgivings, he did his best to act the part of a sophisticate who belonged among Brazil's erudite elite. He had a mission to complete.

It took mere minutes to be ushered onboard. It wasn't like this particular crowd would be accustomed to waiting for anything. Ten minutes later, they cast off and were on their way. The three split off and mingled among the glitterati. Eva was the most at ease, making small talk and issuing compliments, ingratiating herself into knots of partygoers. She was a natural. Again, Nash wondered how accustomed she was to parties like this.

Nnadi's approach was different. It was her graceful aloofness that attracted attention. People wanted to know her story, wanted to know who this Amazonian beauty was. Every time she was asked, she launched into a wild and elaborate back story, each different to the last. It created a buzz among sections of the crowd as partygoers passed on her memoir, no doubt embellishing it with each retelling.

Nash's approach, on the other hand, was more straight-forward. He hung by the bar, eavesdropping, and engaged only when there was a mention of the host, the ship or the organisers of the party.

His approach failed to garner any more information about the architect of the soirée. After an hour, they were no closer to finding the elusive Pace/Sikes, and Nash was beginning to feel the whole Brazilian sojourn had been a waste of time.

Then the DJ interrupted the soft techno with Kenny Loggins' "Danger Zone". The abrupt change in music styles was so jarring, every head turned. Descending the stairs, flanked by four heavily armed security guards, was Leonard Pace. Dressed in a white linen suit, he appeared more suited to a seventies disco than a modern sophisticated cruise. He strode into the crowd, where he was rapturously greeted and gladhanded.

Seeing the man move—the way he walked and held himself—Nash was more convinced than ever that Pace was Sikes. Plastic surgery could erase only so much. The hunch of the shoulders, the arrogance of his step, even the fake laugh were all familiar. Even if Nash knew nothing of plastic surgery, he would have been able to spot Sikes in a crowd. It had to be the same man he'd met in Al Hudaydah.

He touched the button for comms. "It's him."

"You're sure?"

"Absolutely no doubt."

"What's the approach?"

Across the opposite side of the yacht, Nash could see Eva was eying off the security surrounding Sikes. Their plastered-on smiles did nothing to shield their determination and ruthlessness. These were trained professionals hired to do one thing: protect Sikes at all costs.

"The approach? I was thinking this..."

Nash put his drink on the bar and strode directly towards Sikes. Striding across the deck, he carved an express path to his prey. The directness of the action caught the eye of security, who visibly tensed.

"Dude, don't you want to wait?" Eva's voice had a concerned edge to it.

Nnadi chipped in. "I concur, maybe we should wait until—"

"Hey, Sikes."

Nash's target turned from the Arab sheik he was chatting to. On seeing Nash, his eyes went wide. All four security guards reached for their sidearms. It took Sikes a moment to recover from the shock, but when he did, his arms went wide.

"Nash! You son of a bitch!"

Sikes leapt towards Nash, who crouched, ready to defend himself. Embracing Nash in a big bear hug, Sikes lifted him clear off the ground.

It wasn't an offensive move. It was a friendly one.

"Holy shit, dude! It's so awesome to see you!" Sikes released Nash from the hug and bounced from one foot to the other with visible excitement. "This is nuts, oh man. I can't believe you're here." He jovially punched Nash's shoulder as if he didn't know what to do next. "This is so cool. How you doin'? What have you been up to?"

"That..." Eva's voice sounded as confused as Nash was, "was not what I expected."

"Let's grab a drink!"

Sikes looped his arm through Nash's and guided him to the nearest bar. Sikes didn't seem to be putting on an act for the sake of the crowd. He was genuinely excited to see Nash. It only multiplied his confusion.

"I'm going to keep an eye on the situation." The tension in Nnadi's voice didn't seem to have dissipated in line with Nash's.

"I'm with you there. Nash, signal if you want us to step in."

In response, Nash gave his head the slightest of shakes.

"You like my new face? I got it done in South Korea. Cost a bomb, but my guy was the best, I tell you, the best. The recovery was a bitch, but so worth it. Look, look..." Sikes tilted his head up and swivelled so Nash could see all under his chin. "Seamless, right? Absolutely seamless. I tell you, my guy does the best work in the world. You want an espresso martini? Sure you do, everyone does." He waved at the bartender and held up two fingers in case there was any doubt. "Man, like, I knew you were a super spy and all, but my dude, how the hell did you track me down? Don't give me some bullshit story like you just stumbled in here, either." He gave Nash another good-natured punch in the arm. "Man, it's so awesome to see you. Come on, tell me everything."

"I, uh..." Sikes' reaction was so outside what Nash had expected, he was finding it difficult to reply.

If Sikes had sent assassins after him, the natural course of action would be for security to get Nash away from the host as soon as humanly possible. It was doubtful Sikes was trying to save face in front of his guests. All he had to do was claim Nash was a troublemaking party crasher and security would haul him off without anyone batting an eyebrow. What exactly was Sikes' story then?

"Nash, heads up, we got activity."

Eva's warning seemed to align with Nash's thoughts. Perhaps they were intending to haul him away after all.

"Port side. These security guys are more heavily armed. Close-range carbines, webbing, sidearms. They seem different, attack crouches, advancing fast. These guys are the business."

"Starboard side too," Nnadi piped in. "These guys are converging fast. Something's about to go down."

Realising his time may have been running out, Nash turned to Sikes. "What do you know about Tartarus?"

In an instant, all colour drained from Sikes' face. The man appeared to be on the verge of throwing up. Clawing back the ability to speak, he said, "What have you done?" There was genuine fear in Sikes' demeanour. "You haven't brought them here, have you?"

"Who?"

The two security guards flanking Sikes suddenly straightened up and held their fingers to their ears. Their eyes darted about the ship, clear alarm in their eyes.

The one nearest to Nash asked, "Say again?"

Whatever was said again did not please the rough, hulking man. He snapped his fingers, motioning to his counterpart. The gesture was clear: *you're with me.*

He addressed Sikes. "Sir, I'm afraid we have to escort you to safety. There's been a—"

Whatever the end of the sentence was going to be, it was never uttered. The guard's chest exploded.

The bullet struck dead in the centre of his heart, killing him before he could process what had happened. Before his companion had a chance to react, his chest likewise exploded, struck by a bullet as accurate and as deadly as the first. Both bodies dropped to the ground.

There was an odd juxtaposition of sentiments in the crowd. Those closest to Sikes' security team screamed in horror. Those further away, who were oblivious to the commotion, carried on like they were still at a high-end party, laughing and dancing as though people's bodies weren't being blown apart.

"Down!" Nash shoved Sikes' head to the deck.

"Your drinks, gentlemen." The bartender placed two martini glasses on the bar. Realising the two were no longer where they'd stood a second before, he repeated, "Gentlemen?"

Noticing the streaks of red, the bartender removed the mop towel from his belt and wiped down the bar.

Nash yelled at the bartender, "Sniper!"

He searched the upper portions of the ship's structure. They were kilometres from shore, the shots could only have come from onboard.

"Sniper?" The bartender didn't appear at all concerned. "I'll have to ask if we have any butterscotch schnapps."

Before Nash could issue another warning, the nearby daiquiri machine exploded in a torrent of blue and green. The bartender squealed a high-pitched scream and sensibly —if belatedly—ducked behind the bar.

The crowd finally cottoned on to what was happening and the screaming redoubled in earnest. The rest of Sikes' security rallied after their initial flat footedness, extracted their pistols and fired. The more heavily armed black-clad new arrivals returned the favour.

Nnadi's voice came over Nash's earpiece. "Why is Sikes' security team shooting at one another?"

"Incompetence?" Eva offered. "Pay dispute?"

Nash thought it best to go directly to the source. "What the hell is going on?"

Clutching the front of Nash's jacket, Sikes cried, "You brought them here, didn't you?"

"Who?"

"You know exactly who." Sikes' eyes narrowed. "Tartarus. You've killed us all."

As the two groups exchanged gunfire, the crowd did what crowds normally do when panicked: they darted in all directions, assuming anywhere else would be safer than where they currently were. The result was a predictable mayhem.

It was a mayhem Nash used to his advantage. Grabbing the back of Sikes' jacket, he half carried, half shoved the American towards the centre structure of the megayacht. Bouncing off the jostling crowd, Nash pushed him towards cover. If he could get to another deck, there was a chance they could fight their way to the lower sections and find a life raft, a panic room, lifejackets, whatever. Right now, anything was better than being on an open deck in the middle of a firefight.

"Eva, I think we might need that contingency of yours."

"I think so too. Activating now."

His hope was to make their way aft, where they should find a life raft or at least a flotation device. Ideally a jet ski, but he acknowledged that may be too big an ask. Then again, given the surroundings, they might find a fleet of them. But they had to get there first.

In reality, they had only to stay afloat a short amount of time, but right now even that seemed a pipedream. More gunshots and screams came from different decks. The situation was growing more desperate by the second.

Forcing their way towards the main structure and the cabins, Nash extracted the AR-15 Glock Nnadi had supplied. He didn't want to use it, but in a him or them situation, Nash would be forced to choose the former. He hoped it didn't come to that.

That hope was short lived.

From around a corner, one of the heavily armed assailants stepped out, his carbine planted firmly in his shoulder. Pure instinct kicked in, honed over years of training, deadly missions, reflexes ingrained so deeply that actions happened before the thought was even processed. Through pure reflex, Nash unloaded three rounds into the dead centre of the man's chest. He reeled backwards amid the screams of the passengers.

As the man fell, Nash glared forlornly. "Sorry, man. Sorry. Shit."

Nash had to admit the fallen assailant likely cared little for the apology. Doing his best to push down the distaste and revulsion at his actions, Nash relied on his training, rather than focusing on the consequences of using it. He readied his aim for the next target, hoping desperately not to find one. He swept to the opposite side of the boat, not knowing how many assailants he was dealing with.

"Uh, Nash." Sikes tapped him on the shoulder.

He turned to see that the assailant he'd shot was not only standing, but his gun was aimed directly at them.

"Oh, thank god."

Sikes reeled in horror. "What?!"

Pushing Sikes away, Nash dove to the deck and rolled. He loosed more rounds as he did, all going wide as he hadn't taken time to aim properly. His opposition didn't fare any better; his shots followed Nash, but they were rushed and undisciplined.

Taking cover behind a pylon, Nash swung his pistol hand left and fired blindly. It was a feint; he rolled to the right and fired with better targeted shots. His shots were not aimed at the assailant, just near enough that his foe would think they were. It also meant Nash was now out of ammo.

The result was exactly what Nash wanted. The assailant fired back, likewise expending his ammunition.

Nash leapt from his cover and sprinted. The goon's clip swap procedure was smooth and well-honed. He chambered a round and pivoted towards the rapidly advancing blur. Unfortunately for him, Nash got there first. Before the assailant fired, Nash grasped the top of the slide and held firm while pushing down. The bullet splintered the wooden deck. But the damage was done.

The assailant shouldered him away and Nash accommodated the move. A smug sneer crossed the opponent's face. He raised his pistol and pulled the trigger. Nothing happened.

Maybe this guy's not so heavily trained. Nash knew from experience that restricting the slide while firing jammed most pistols.

The assailant's gaze moved towards his jammed gun and Nash leapt forward, landing a right hook square on his jaw. As he staggered back, Nash advanced, alternating left and right punches as his opponent fell. The final right cross felt like Nash was punching right through the floor. The goon was out by the time his head heavily collided with the deck.

Shaking his aching fists, Nash turned to Sikes. "Bullet-proof vests. High-end gear. Who the hell are these guys?"

"I told you," Sikes gulped, "Tartarus. We're fucked."

"Heads up," Eva cautioned in his ear. "One incoming to your position. Port side."

Instead of reloading his own weapon, Nash bounded towards the nearest wall and tore off a fire extinguisher. Pulling the pin to break the seal, he aimed the nozzle towards the corner Eva had advised. So far, none of the assault troops wore protective goggles or masks. That suited Nash's purposes, but it also meant that whoever they were, they didn't care if their faces were seen. It didn't exactly bode well for the passengers.

The unmasked head of a heavily armed assailant poked around the corner and Nash squeezed the fire extinguisher, releasing a fountain of white chemicals to engulf the goon. Instinctively, the assailant's hand went to wipe the foreign material from his face. In the fraction of a second he managed to restore his vision, he would have seen the butt of a fire extinguisher coming straight for him. The blow knocked his head back and was soon followed by two more. Like his comrade, he too was unconscious before his head hit the deck.

Nash scanned the area, but there didn't appear to be any immediate threats in the vicinity. Tossing the extinguisher aside, he turned to Sikes. "What the hell is going on? Are these bastards after you or me?"

Sikes' face smacked of fear. "Both, I assume."

Nash's eyes narrowed. "Both?"

Sikes shook his head. "After you saved me in Al-Jamadi I've done things I regret." His face was despondent. "I'll regret them until my dying day."

"I don't think you're going to live that long." The new voice came from behind.

Nash closed his eyes as his shoulders slumped. "I know that voice."

In his ear, Eva asked, "Who is it?"

"Nobody I particularly want to hang out with, if I'm completely honest."

"Hello, Mason," the new voice growled. "So glad you could make it."

Nash turned to see the familiar shape step from the shadows. He moved a fraction of an inch towards the last assailant's pistol, which lay near his feet, but the new arrival tutted and jiggled his pistol towards Nash. It was a clear warning: he knew what Nash was thinking, and he'd be dead if he tried.

"I've been meaning to catch up..." Pinchot gave a slanted grin, his missing tooth now firmly back in place, "old friend."

CHAPTER
ELEVEN

Nash was roughly thrown to the deck. A second later Sikes landed awkwardly beside him on the expensive wooden floor. Both had zip ties fastening their hands in front of them. The deck was empty except for the two prisoners and the four heavily armed goons assigned to watch them.

Nash folded his legs into a lotus pose and focused on his breath work. He could have wet himself instead, but Sikes had beaten him to it and he didn't want to seem like a copycat.

For some inexplicable reason, three large movie cameras were now on deck, as if someone was making a big-budget movie. What their purpose was, Nash had no idea. Another thing he had no idea about was where the rest of the guests were.

Pinchot had gone off to coordinate the takeover of the ship, leaving his thugs with orders to shoot to kill should Nash or Sikes make a move. They'd both been searched thoroughly.

Although not thoroughly enough. Nash still had his comms device.

In a low voice, he asked, "Eva, Nnadi, you there?"

Nash glanced up to the guards ten metres away. Two faced outward, watching for any threats, while the other two faced them with menacing intent. Nash faced Sikes as he spoke, hoping the guards would assume he was talking to his fellow captive.

"Yeah, we're here." Eva's voice was low and muffled. "We're on the third deck, in a closet, like that's going to make a difference. They seem to be doing sweeps room by room. We're more screwed than a groupie on a Black Sabbath tour bus. It's only a matter of time, I'm afraid. Like Sister Mary Margarette used to say in Sunday school, we're royally fucked, Nash."

He sniggered. "I can't imagine you ever attending Sunday school."

"I don't think that's our focus right now." In the background, Nash heard Nnadi utter something unintelligible. Eva went on. "How is Pinchot here? You told Paul you killed him."

"No, I never told Paul that."

"Like fuck. You said it to me."

"No, you claimed I killed him, I just never corrected you. I'm not a killer anymore, I'm a pacifist. Why must I keep repeating myself?"

"You just walloped that guy." Sikes pointed to the body on the ground. "And that one. If you're a pacifist, you're really shit at it, dude."

Nash was in no mood to argue. Sikes knew he was capable of far more lethal means of taking down the opposition, but had actively chosen not to employ them, even while under fire. It wasn't ideal, but it was the best he could do given the circumstances.

It was the reason Pinchot still drew breath. After concluding the interrogation, Nash had administered Propofol to knock him out, then proceeded to haul his limp body to the nearest hospital. Taking him inside was out of the question; instead, he'd dragged the body out of the boot of the car and placed it in a nearby side street. He'd used a burner phone to call the hospital and advised them he'd seen an unconscious man in the street. The burner phone was then tossed out the window.

Through his earpiece, Nash heard thumping on a door, followed by unintelligible shouting.

Nash sucked in salty air. "Eva, unarm yourselves."

"What?"

"They don't know who you are. If you don't fight back they'll think you're simply another couple of guests. You can still get out of this."

"Ballbags. But you're—"

The shouting around Eva intensified.

"My fate is my own. Save yourselves. Fighting back will only get you killed."

Nash heard muffled movement and the distinct *click* of weaponry.

Eva sighed, defeat in her voice. "I'd feel better shooting something."

"I hear you, but given the odds, this is the only way for you two to get out alive."

"But I *really* want to shoot someone."

In spite of everything, Nash smiled. Through his earpiece he heard a crack of wood and women screaming; Eva and Nnadi playing the part of terrified guests. Through panicked screeches they did a plausible act of petrified partygoers who had no idea what was going on. They were ushered out—roughly, by the sounds of the grunts—and then ordered to follow someone.

Nash gave a sigh of relief. If the two MI6 agents got out, he'd consider it a win. He held no illusions as to the fate of Sikes and himself, but at least he could die knowing his companions had a decent chance of survival.

That, it turned out, was false hope.

Pinchot strode onto the deck like the proverbial cat that got the proverbial cream. He was dressed in a white tuxedo, indicating he'd somehow made it onboard before his assault troops. His bow tie was undone and hanging freely from his neck.

"Gentlemen." Pinchot tilted his head theatrically as he observed Nash's cross-legged form. "Are we doing yoga?"

Nash unfolded his legs. "I'd be happy to show you the corpse pose, Jack."

Chuckling mirthlessly, Pinchot said, "You look lonely, let me remedy that for you."

He clicked his fingers. Four of his heavily armed troops dragged in a writhing, bare-footed Eva and Nnadi and roughly deposited them at Pinchot's feet. Unlike Sikes and Nash, their hands were unbound. No other guests joined them.

Oh hell.

Pinchot took great pleasure in seeing Nash's reaction. He rocked on his heels.

"What's with the white tuxedo?" Eva asked, glaring at Pinchot.

"You like it?" He smoothed down a lapel.

Eva turned away. "I guess if the vibe you were going for was a yacht-rock listening middle-aged twat."

"Charming, Ms Destruction. Your reputation seems

accurate. I'll deal with you momentarily." Pinchot sighed and turned his attention to Nnadi. He spoke without the aid of notes. "Ms Hadiza Nnadi, born 1994. Spent her adolescence with her diplomat father in St Petersburg. Graduated University of Oxford 2019, with honours, no less. Well done you. Joined MI6 that same year, placed in an accelerated program under Amanda Bridgeman, then assigned first field op in August 2020, where she—"

"How do you know all this?"

Pinchot laughed at Nash. "Because we're more formidable and have better intelligence than the CIA and MI6 combined. Tartarus is all powerful, all knowing." He sneered maliciously. "We're omnipotent, omniscient and omnipresent."

"Sounds like a God delusion to me."

"Yes, yes, God is a good analogy." Pinchot chuckled in amusement. "You're absolutely right." His countenance took on a far more sinister air. He tilted his head as he extracted a pistol from his shoulder holster. "Like God, we have control over life and death itself."

Without another word, he aimed his pistol at the side of Nnadi's head and pulled the trigger. The young woman's brains were blown out the side of her skull.

Eva and Nash cried out at the same instant, "No!"

With hands bound, Nash crumpled to the deck. In front of him, Eva rushed to Nnadi's side. She knew how fruitless the gesture was. No one survived a brutal headshot like that. Clutching at the body, Eva wailed, then shot Pinchot a venomous glance.

"I'll fucking kill you. I'm going to rip your head off and give you a spine-dectomy. That's not a fucking euphemism, that's exactly what I'm going to do, you cockless wankstain on humanity."

Seeing Eva in such a state, Nash did the only thing he could think of to stave off the inevitable. He addressed Pinchot.

"You just murdered a member of MI6."

Pinchot held up his hands in a *you got me* gesture, as if someone had accused him of littering. "C'est la vie. I had my reasons."

"You can't just throw out a German phrase and dismiss it."

Pinchot gave a half shake of his head. "It's... it's French."

"You will pay for that."

"No. I won't. Here's the thing, Mason. I'm not afraid of MI6, or the CIA. Mossad. SVR RF. None of them. You know why? Because no intelligence agency is a threat to us. We're beyond their reach. We're more powerful, more agile and more dangerous than you could possibly imagine."

The same thought kept reverberating around Nash's mind. *Keep him talking. Keep him talking.* He understood it was a futile effort, but he had no other cards to play.

"Are you going to kill everyone onboard?"

The question was generic, but it was mainly about Eva. He still had no doubt about Sikes' fate, or his own.

"Of course not. We're not the bad guys here. They're all downstairs enjoying canapés and champagne. See these cameras?" Pinchot pointed to the three large machines that had been deposited on deck. "We're going to tell the guests they've been part of an elaborate movie shoot. It's all been a ploy to get genuine reactions on film and to give them a hell of a story to take home. Joel here," he pointed to one of his henchmen, "has been rigged up with squibs to simulate gunshots. We'll show them, and they'll love it. The party will go on and this will be the most exciting thing ever to happen in their privileged little lives."

On the port side, one of Sikes' remaining guards, perhaps the last one, burst from a bulkhead, firing a pistol in each hand. Pinchot's goons turned and fired. The man didn't even make it past the hatch. He was mown down in a bloody barrage.

With the guards distracted, Eva stood and sprinted in the opposite direction. She was surprisingly fast in her bare feet. In only a few bounds, she'd made good ground. It took a second for Nash to realise she wasn't heading back to the superstructure, but perpendicular to it.

"Eva, no!"

She didn't listen. Eva Destruction dove over the railing and into the black. If the fall didn't kill her, the churning pitch-black sea would.

The entire deck stood in awed silence. Nobody moved. Nobody could.

"Did she just..." Pinchot nervously laughed. "We're in the middle of the ocean! My god, she's insane." Pinchot jogged to the railing and peered over. He searched the ocean, but seemingly didn't see a trace of her.

Nash couldn't drag his eyes away from the gap Eva had disappeared into. She'd done it. She'd leapt the equivalent of three storeys into the South Atlantic Ocean.

Sikes glared at the railing, slack-jawed. "It has to be, what, tens of miles to land." He shook his head. "Even the most experienced marathon swimmers would drown long before they saw shore, especially in the middle of the night, with no support, wearing a fucking evening gown." He turned to Nash. "She would have known she was going to die, but she did it anyway. What the actual hell?"

"Go back!" Nash realised how unhinged he sounded. "Turn around and get her!"

Still amused by the situation, Pinchot shook his head.

"You, buddy, are in no position to make demands." Pinchot walked back to Sikes and Nash. "The silly girl. I wasn't going to kill her."

"You killed her partner!"

Pinchot sighed. "That's because she was a double agent, Mason. A deception your ex-organisation should have discovered long ago, quite frankly. She's been dealing with the Russians under the table for as long as she's been at MI6. Her handler in Moscow has been pressuring her to get a posting in Washington. They're extremely insistent, if the communications are anything to go by."

Nash recalled Nnadi saying she was angling for a Washington posting, so that part sounded plausible. Or did it? None of this was making sense.

Trying to stave off the image of Eva diving overboard, Nash said, "But you killed all those people tonight?"

"Who did we kill? There were no civilian casualties. We're not monsters, Mason. All the guards Sikes here hired are Comando Vermelho. These are not nice men. All of them have been involved in drug and arms trafficking, protection racketeering, kidnappings-for-ransom, armoured truck hijackings, narco-terrorism, you name it. We've done the world a service here tonight, believe me." He glowered at Sikes, who sat at his feet, then placed a finger under his chin so the terrified American had no choice but to look up. "Speaking of such things, whatever shall we do with you? We gave you everything and you betrayed us. So disappointing."

"I, see, I, it's...You wouldn't let me leave. I panicked. I had—"

"You," Pinchot brutally cut him off, "are an ungrateful little turd. I saved your fucking worthless life and what did you do for us in return?"

"But the things you made me do..."

Pinchot waved a dismissive hand. "Save it. You'll have plenty of time to grovel. We're taking you back to the compound."

"No, I..."

"You what? Want to hold onto all the wealth you stole from us? No, I don't think so."

Pinchot clicked his fingers and motioned to Sikes. Seconds later, he was hoisted up and carried away, out of sight.

Nash was alone, unarmed and in the most hostile environment he could imagine. Fun times.

Striding lazily to a nearby chair, Pinchot carried it back and sat in front of Nash. As he casually crossed his legs, he shook his head.

"What ever shall we do with *you*, my dear Mason?"

Poking his chin towards his nemesis, Nash asked, "How's the tooth?"

Pinchot chuckled. "That's what you want to know? It's fine, thank you."

"No hard feelings then?"

Instead of seeming incensed, Pinchot chuckled. "For what? Ripping out my tooth? The countless hours of torture? Why on earth would I have hard feelings, old friend?"

Nash shrugged. "I did drop you off at a hospital."

Pinchot held up a finger. "*Near* a hospital. Minus a tooth."

"Uh, I preserved them in milk, thank you very much. Teeth last hours in milk. You could thank me."

The amiable façade finally crumbled. "You almost killed me!"

It was the first crack in his calm demeanour. Pinchot

was nowhere near as calm as he made out to be.

"Almost." Nash tilted his head to the side. "But I didn't. I could have easily, but I chose not to."

"This newfound non-violent business of yours is truly a fluid thing, isn't it?" Pinchot rubbed his jaw. "I must say, you've done well. You got far further than my colleagues thought you would. You should be commended."

"Commended? What do you mean?"

"The way you took down the three assassins we hired, and hell, you avoided a god-damn gunship! You found our clue in the laptop and managed to find Sikes when even we couldn't. You impressed our board no end, Nash. That's no easy task, believe me."

"What, you left a clue...?" Head spinning, Nash was trying to keep up. "If you left a clue, then why send assassins? Unless they weren't trying to kill me?"

"Oh, they really were. Paid a ridiculous price, by the way. Plus, you can't exactly take out insurance on assassins, so we had to pay their employer an absolute fortune for what you did." He held up his hands in a *that's life* gesture. "But we laid out some breadcrumbs in case they failed in their mission. You managed to find them all, and they led you all the way here. The way you conducted my interrogation, it was a flawless performance, I have to say, even though I was the recipient. In my books, this is not someone past their prime. You still torture like a pro, Nash."

This was certainly an odd change in conversation. Was Pinchot complimenting him on his torture technique? The torture technique that had inflicted countless hours of horrific pain and brought Pinchot so close to death?

"Look, I'm into kink as much as the next person, Jack, but that's—"

Pinchot clapped his hands together, indicating he did

not wish to be interrupted. "All these things were most impressive for an ex-spy who seems to be under the misapprehension he's out of the game. You've still got it, my not so old friend. The fact that you're even here breathing is a testament to your skills as an espionage agent. You should be applauded."

"I... applauded...? What the hell are you on about?"

Pinchot chuckled mirthlessly. "I mean, you obviously still have it. We could use skills, talents and experience like yours. Everything you've done over the last couple of weeks has persuaded the board to offer you a position."

Nash head spun. "A position where, exactly?"

Pinchot smiled. "With Tartarus, of course."

CHAPTER
TWELVE

Nash named the biggest one Geoffrey.

The challengers he named Bartholomew, Theodore and Gary. Gary was the dark horse. Just as the three aggressors made their move, Nash was rudely interrupted by a knock at the door.

Sighing, he yelled, "What is it?"

There was a jangle of keys and the heavy wooden door creaked open. A seemingly familiar thick-necked goon with a black eye stood impatiently in the doorway. Nash thought it might be rude to ask the guard if he was the heavily armed assailant Nash had taken down with nothing more than a fire extinguisher. Thugs were generally upset when you brought up such things.

The thug spoke with a gravelly intensity. "Mr Pinchot..." His gaze wandered to where Nash sat at the end of his bed. "What are you doing?"

Nash pointed at the far wall. "I'm watching these cockroaches fight and wondering who will be the victor." He bared his teeth at his captor. "It's really rather thrilling."

The thug stared at him for the longest time. Nash waited.

For a cell, the room had a lovely view. Although recently renovated, with modern fixtures, a lush bathroom and a comfortable bed, there was no hiding the old stonework and cramped feel of an ancient fortress. Situated above a high ocean cliff, it was impossible to determine which country he was in. Judging by the length of the helicopter trip Nash had taken while a hood covered his head, he estimated they were still in South America, but he couldn't hazard a guess as to where.

The thug finally managed to break the silence. "Mr Pinchot requests your presence in the grand hall."

"Requests, you say?"

"Yes."

"That's very polite."

"It is."

"And if I refuse?"

"Then I have orders to take you there anyway."

"Ah." Nash nodded. "So, it's less a polite request and more an order."

"Take it any way you like." For effect, the thug cracked his knuckles and glared at Nash as if he'd love nothing more than crush his skull with his bare hands. "But you're coming whether you like it or not."

Nash did not. But as the big oaf, who clearly held a grudge against the man who'd beaned him with a fire extinguisher, had said, he didn't have much of a choice. He stood and motioned for the thug to lead the way.

For three days Nash had been held captive in the fortress. In that time, he'd seen nine helicopter supply runs, twice-daily training exercises in the main compound and patrols every fifteen minutes. He estimated twenty guards, at least the same again in support staff, plus another dozen or so who walked with the arrogance of senior leadership. This wasn't a fly-by-night small scale operation. *Who the hell are these guys?*

Nash had the distinct impression he was about to find out.

The grand hall didn't exactly live up to its name, at least not size-wise. No larger than three or four regular dining rooms, the hall made up for its lack of size in sheer ostentatiousness. The gold embossed roof was merely the beginning. The walls were a red velvet, the subdued lighting cast by expensive chandeliers. All it needed was a grand piano and Liberace would have felt right at home.

"What time does the floor show start?"

Pinchot glanced up from his position at the dining table, closed his laptop and grinned. "I hope the accommodation is to your liking?"

Nash ignored the question. "Did anyone find Eva?"

"No. Then again, no one has been searching for her." Pinchot didn't seem to take any pride in this fact. "No reports of a body washing up anywhere in the last few days, if that's what you're asking. But it's a vast ocean, it's unlikely the body will ever show up." He shook his head. "It's a shame, she could have been a great asset to the organisation."

"You'd shot her colleague."

"Her *traitorous* colleague. She jumped overboard before I had a chance to explain it to her."

"You never gave her the chance."

"I wanted to. She's had an incredible career for one so young. Did you ever read any of her missions? You could write a series of books about her exploits. Such a waste."

"Having spent the last couple of days lamenting her

passing, I'm not about to argue." In his head, Nash had played out her leap into the abyss a thousand times, and imagined another thousand times how it could have been prevented.

Casting his sorrowful eyes downward, Pinchot said nothing. At least he had the good sense to know when to remain silent.

Unable to help himself, Nash asked the question that was burning within him. "Just what is this organisation? What is Tartarus?"

Leaning back in his chair, Pinchot motioned for Nash to sit opposite him at the table. Before he'd taken his place, Pinchot launched into his pitch.

"The CIA is bloated, bureaucratic and above all else, visible. Every move it makes is scrutinised by Congress, debated endlessly in the press. That kind of scrutiny makes an organisation gun shy, which it has been for decades, avoidant of anything with even a whiff of risk. It's become a swollen, slow, toothless beast no one has the heart to put out of its misery."

Nash didn't interrupt. The delivery seemed well-rehearsed.

"Sounds a lot like good old MI6, doesn't it? A distended corpse of an organisation, feeding off its past glories while trying convince the world it's still relevant. Have I stated anything inaccurate so far?"

Shaking his head, Nash gestured for Pinchot to go on.

"That's why Tartarus exists. A secret service organisation that's actually *secret*. Beyond the oversight of self-interested populist leaders who know nothing of the world of espionage. It was designed to be what Truman originally envisaged the CIA to be, not the bloated PR company it turned into."

"So this is all government run?"

Based on the activities he'd witnessed, including and not limited to an armed assault on a civilian yacht, Nash doubted Tartarus had any government oversight. Unless that government was insane.

Pinchot clasped his hands together. "Initially. Our private security organisation began as secretly government-funded, yes. We're comprised of elite past members of the CIA, MI6, Mossad and the DGSE. Our stealth enables us to remove targets before they strike. We were originally given hundreds of millions of dollars to set up a network across the globe. Untraceable to its source, we're now self-sustaining." He spread his arms wide. "We are a global cabal of ex-intelligence elite."

"Self-sustaining? As in, you make money?"

Pinchot waggled his eyebrows, amused at the question. "We were quietly set up by a previous US president. The fact that we were designed to be a profit generating independent organisation no doubt tells you which president. We generate enough revenue to not only sustain ourselves, but to expand our operation. We're able to operate rapidly and assertively, never bogged down by Congress or bureaucracy. A dynamic and flexible intelligence organisation, able to respond decisively to any threat."

"And subsequent administrations are okay with this?"

Pinchot dropped a coy schoolboy simper. "Well, the thing is, the US government lost control of us quite some time ago. To be completely transparent, they don't know where we've gone. As far as they know, Tartarus simply vanished."

"Surely the CIA has been after you? I hardly think they'll accept the disappearance of a stealth intelligence organisation."

"That's the thing, they barely knew of our existence in the first place. Not many did. The initial funding came from a significant increase in the black budget, but with no real details. Very few had access to the content of the charter or budget, so there was hardly anyone to query where the money went. And those few who did know have no idea where we've gone. Let's be honest here, shall we? If you were responsible for a private espionage organisation that you'd lost track of, would you tell a soul? I think not."

For Nash, the very thought of an independent spy agency was horrifying. Oversight was what kept any one organisation from going too far, stopped any unelected leader with delusions of grandeur from seizing more power than they deserved. It prevented wars.

The notion of a powerful, unaccountable organisation was nightmare fuel. In the wrong hands, an organisation with this amount of extraordinary supremacy could be catastrophic. That much power in anyone's hands was already the wrong hands.

"Who controls all this?"

"Who holds us accountable? We have a board. I'm on it, and six others. We hold Tartarus on the true path, ensure we are a force for good in the world."

Nash sneered. "Good is subjective."

Frowning in acceptance of the statement, Pinchot continued. "Maybe it is, maybe it isn't. Tell me, is human trafficking good?"

"No."

"Forced prostitution, slavery?"

"Obviously—"

"What about a regime set on pillaging, raping and murdering their conquests? One that mutates captives by removing limbs and ears and noses, leaving nothing but barren farmland laden with boobytraps for generations to come to start the maiming all over again. Would you call that *good*?"

Nash clenched his fists. "Alright, fine. Even if I believed the fairytale about a benevolent secret service agency, one that's all lollipops, rainbows and death squads for only the bad people. Even if I pretend that's possible, who's to say it can't be corrupted? It can all be manipulated. It can be bent into something more sinister and evil."

"There's an easy way to prevent that from happening." Pinchot's eyes flared. "Become part of it."

Nash sat up. "What?"

"Become part of Tartarus."

"I thought you were bullshitting back on the ship. In case you forgot, you tried to kill me at Devil's End."

Pinchot waved his hand dismissively. "You were the only one who could connect Sikes and myself. We both reported him dead to our respective organisations, remember? Your man Hearn died two months after the mission in a light plane crash in Eritrea." He held up his hands. "Not our doing. It was well before we were even formed. And my man Travis now works for us."

"But Sikes left you months ago, why attack me now?"

"A fair question. He stole from us when he left. No doubt knowing we'd use all our resources to track him down, he used the funds to change his appearance and create a new personality. But he got greedy. After a couple of months his money obviously began to run out, so he started pilfering more of our assets. Did you see the ship he bought? Idiot. That was our money he bought it with. I'm surprised you found him before we did, to be honest. Sikes." He shook his head. "Some fools are just born lucky."

"I'm not sure he'd agree with your assessment there."

Pinchot went on. "Because we hadn't found him, we feared he'd eventually garner the attention of other government-run organisations. If they found him and drew the connection between us, this organisation would be over before we began. That, we just couldn't allow. Up until that time we'd spared you, despite what you knew. But with Sikes a loose cannon, we had to act decisively."

"By which you mean kill me."

Pinchot gave a schoolboy grin. "You, my dear Mason, were the only one not in Tartarus who knew Sikes was alive. The only one who could bring this all down on our heads. You were a loose thread that needed snipping."

"And here you are offering me a job." Nash rubbed the back of his neck. "To be honest, I can't even believe we're having an amicable conversation. I tortured you, Jack. How are you even speaking to me civilly?"

Pinchot frowned, amused. "I'm not holding a grudge, if that's what you're asking."

"No?"

"No."

"What about putting it somewhere handy. Keeping it nearby?"

Pinchot's face crumpled into confusion. "What?"

"If you're not holding a grudge you could be keeping it close by, just for emergencies."

Chuckling, Pinchot shook his head. "No, nothing like that."

"In a locked trunk?"

"Is it really so hard to believe a torture victim can forgive the torturer?"

"Well, frankly, yes."

Pinchot waved a dismissive hand. "We're professionals, we know how to move on. That's what I've done, otherwise

I wouldn't be offering you a job. Like I said, you've since proven yourself more than worthy. Let's be honest, shall we? I know you're ready for this. If I came to you weeks ago when you were but a humble history teacher pretending to be happily retired, would you have been contemplating the offer the way you are now?"

"Who says I'm contemplating it?"

Pinchot leaned forward. "Look at the state of the world, Mason. I mean, really look at it. World politics is without a rudder, without direction. The halcyon days of the US being the world's global policeman are long gone. Once, the great powers of Europe, the British Empire, the United States, the USSR, were the guiding forces. These days Russia is busy struggling to hold onto its Communist-lite dictatorship while America is doing its best to plunge itself into another civil war. Even in our lifetime, you remember Middle-East peace deals, admittedly doomed, were brokered by the great powers. Who can perform the task now? The UN is toothless, the European Union is too busy regulating milk products, there is no guiding hand. There is no force for good. No one is doing what's *right*."

"And what is right, according to Tartarus?"

"We take down the evil dictatorships who encourage their soldiers to rape and murder their own people. Cut off the heads of those who run the slave trade. Make sure the rich oligarchs who make their fortunes exploiting of the poorest in the world are held accountable for their crimes, instead of showered with presidential dinners because they fund ridiculously expensive party campaigns. Taking action against these people is not evil. It needs an organisation with the will to carry them out." He waved his hands around the room. "And the means."

Nash spun his table knife in circles on the tablecloth. "I'm going to have to think about this."

Pinchot gave him a sage nod. "You have until sundown."

"What happens at sundown?"

"We have dinner."

NASH STARED up at the ceiling of his new "guest accommodation" cell. It wasn't gold embossed, though that mattered little, as he wasn't pondering the ceiling at all. His mind churned with a million other thoughts.

They had moved him to a better room to contemplate the offer, one with fewer cockroaches. When they did so, he finally got a good look at Tartarus headquarters. The ancient clifftop fort overlooked a vast ocean. Inside its high stone walls were lush, manicured green hills, and neat concrete paths provided a softer, more tourist-friendly touch. There was a motor pool, helipad, barracks for at least a few dozen personnel. It was all neat and well maintained. It was a like a PG13 fortress: big and foreboding, but, according to the guard who showed Nash to his room, it came complete with a sauna, Michelin star chefs and a weekly karaoke competition.

He doubted Tartarus could be the benevolent organisation Pinchot made it out to be. No organisation could. Sure, there had been plenty of times throughout his career when Nash had bemoaned the government's inability to act in what he thought was the right way—but that was the problem. What *he* thought was the right way. What if he was wrong, and the path he wanted in a moment of hot-headedness was actually the incorrect one? That was precisely the reason there were failsafe mechanisms, higher-ups far smarter than Nash who made those calls. As much as grunts on the ground like him bemoaned their inability to make the big decisions, deep down, most were glad they didn't.

Was he wrong?

Was it possible Tartarus could be a force for good? What if everything Pinchot had stated was true and they could make a positive impact on the world and eliminate some evil from it? It was an enticing notion. An unrestricted noble power who protected the weak and the defenceless and dispatched the vile and wicked. It was tempting.

While he contemplated all these things, he was certain of something else. There was no doubt the "decision" he had to make was a one-sided one. Nash knew there was only one way this could go. If he chose not to become part of Tartarus, they wouldn't be inclined to tell him no hard feelings, shake his hand and drop him off at home with a word of thanks and a cut lunch. That's not how this was going to play out.

Nash was part of Tartarus, whether he liked it or not.

Now all he had to do was figure out whether he did. He checked his watch. Sundown was less than an hour away. And so was his one-sided decision.

CHAPTER

THIRTEEN

"I'm in," Nash said before the waiter poured the first drink.

"That's marvellous." Pinchot clapped his hands together. He swivelled to Sikes and said, "Isn't that marvellous, Tyler?"

"Yeah." Sikes gulped down the wine the waiter poured and waggled his glass for a refill. "Fantastic. I'm over the fucking moon." He guzzled another, clearly determined to be plastered before the main course.

The three sat in the grand hall around the equally grand table. Pinchot continued to perform his affable host routine. Nash was sure it was all an act. No one was as repeatedly happy to see a former torturer as Pinchot made out to be, no matter how much he wanted Nash to be part of Tartarus.

There was no doubt about Sikes' opinion on the matter. Nash would do his best to use the man's singular mission of inebriation to his advantage—until Sikes passed out, that was.

"So, Sikes. You're obviously critical to the operation

here. Your friend Pinchot went to a great amount of effort to bring you back into the fold. What is it you do exactly?"

Pinchot gave a polite cough. "There will be plenty of time to become familiar with our operation, Mason..."

There was reluctance in his manner. It was clear to Nash he wasn't trusted yet. He wondered how long it would take.

"I'm part of Tartarus now, aren't I? I would have thought joining would convey a certain level of faith in my intentions. Or have I got that wrong, old friend?"

It was obvious Pinchot realised what Nash was doing, but his hand gesture told him to proceed anyway. Nash turned to the plump American.

"He's not your friend." Sikes' delivery was deadpan with a hint of disdain.

Raising an eyebrow, Nash asked, "What's that?"

"Pinchot." Sikes' eyes narrowed on the man across from him. "He's not your friend. He's certainly not mine."

"Now, now, Sikes," Pinchot gave his best gameshow host leer, "is that any way to speak of the man who saved your life back in the day?" He took a polite sip of his wine. "It seems to me you were living quite the life over in Brazil..."

That told Nash they were no longer in Brazil, but gave no indication as to what country they were actually in.

"We gave you a second chance. Wealth. Everything you desired. Remember those twins? All the resources you asked for, and how did you repay us? By absconding with the church funds. Hardly the thanks I would have expected."

"Thanks!" Even the waiter turned at the vehemence with which Sikes spat the word. "Thanks? You *used* me. All this," he waved his arms around the room, "is because of me. I keep your shitshow going. It would be nothing if not for me."

"And you were well compensated for it." Pinchot was becoming increasingly nervous. It was obvious he was scared Sikes would go on a rant in front of his new recruit. "If I am being completely honest—"

"That'd be a first."

"— I'm somewhat disappointed you felt the need to flee from us when we'd provided you so much. Not even a word of farewell or thanks. And that last theft was just rubbing salt into the wound."

Nash didn't believe Pinchot's mock offence for one moment. It was clear they needed Sikes' ingenuity. The hacker had been recruited by Qasim and aided the downing of an airliner. He wasn't exactly the kind of person one would choose to associate with, unless you really had to. Sikes claimed Pinchot and Tartarus used him to generate the funds to keep the operation running, and Nash had no reason to question that. The fact that they hijacked a boat and manipulated Nash to find him showed exactly how much they needed the flawed American.

"Now I'm an employee," Nash did his best to sound friendly and at ease, "do I get a corporate mug? A polo shirt? A laptop?"

He had no real desire for a coffee mug, and in truth, he'd prefer to drink a warm glass of asparagus piss than wear a corporate polo shirt. What Nash really wanted was the laptop.

"No communication with the outside world." Pinchot's gameshow host leer returned. "At least, not yet."

"But how will I know who wins Eurovision? Denmark is really in with a chance this year."

Chuckling, Pinchot did a reasonable impersonation of a

genial employer, though the hardening around the eyes was a tell. "In time, my friend, in time. Like all our new recruits, we want to ensure you are as loyal as you claim." He held up a defensive hand. "Nothing personal, we do the same for everyone who joins our little enterprise. I know this will be a shock to you, but those employed in espionage sometimes don't tell the truth. I was as shocked as anyone when I found this out. In time, the trust will come, believe me."

Unsure if he would ever trust the former CIA operative, Nash intended to find out more about his new employer. "A spy agency that makes money, hey? How exactly does that work?"

"We're not here to make money." Pinchot shook his head. "We fund our little operation to keep fighting the good fight."

"And how do you do that, exactly?"

"Tartarus obtains its operating revenue by keeping the ill-gotten gains by those evildoers we eradicate when others don't have the courage or the capability."

"Did you seriously just use 'evildoers' in a sentence?"

Undeterred by Nash's sarcasm, Pinchot continued to speak as if he was explaining the simplest concept to a toddler. "Normal spy agencies are content with closing the case and allowing the complicit bank to keep the ill-gotten gains of their illicit clientele, or else it goes into government coffers to fund politician pay rises and interpretive dance studios." He held his palms out. "We simply channel their accounts into ours, then give it to the genius Sikes here to reinvest and subsidise our takedown of the next bad guy. It's all well-ordered and efficient," his eyes narrowed on Sikes, "when everyone plays their part."

It was a reasonable explanation and answered some of

Nash's questions, but Nash knew it was unlikely to be as clear-cut as all that.

"So you're telling me you're not in this for the money? This place is decked out with luxury fittings, all staff seem to have the latest weapons, nice outfits. This meal, the wine, all A-grade stuff. I'm hearing helicopters every hour. None of this is cheap."

Pinchot gave a schoolboy shrug.

"And did I see a Lamborghini out there?" Nash motioned towards the motor pool, where a handful of military-style motorbikes and vehicles were parked neatly alongside one very civilian one.

"You mean the great big orange penis compensation?" Sikes hiccupped.

Nash ignored him. "Is that Lambo an ill-gotten gain from one of those evildoers?"

Pinchot shook his head. "No, it's mine."

"My, don't we like to travel incognito?"

"It's my little toy. My pride and joy. I've dreamt of owning a car like that since I was a child. One is allowed to indulge when you're in the private sector, as you'll soon discover."

"He fucken loves that car." Sikes moaned. "Never takes anyone else in it. I've asked, a lot. He gets pissed if you even look at it wrong."

Pinchot tutted Sikes to shut him up. The two glared at one another momentarily. Nash thought it best to move on.

"What happens, I wonder," Nash stated casually, "when you don't have enough bad guys to keep the lights on? How far do your exalted good intentions extend then? How far do those high morals stretch if you start living pay cheque to pay cheque?"

Pinchot gave a little chuckle. "Luckily, or rather unluckily, we have enough rich bad guys to keep us busy."

It was clear there was more to the story than Pinchot was letting on. Nash turned to the other man at the table. Technically, the American getting steadily drunker beside Nash was an actually certified genius. The Tartarus organisation was not yet so self-sufficient it could survive without Sikes' brilliance. Sending hit squads to bring him back proved that all too well.

Before he could travel too far down that line of thinking, Travis walked into the room. The man nodded to Nash in acknowledgement of their brief time in Al Hudaydah. Nash still didn't know if Travis was his first or last name.

The newcomer leaned down and whispered in Pinchot's ear. The former CIA operative removed the napkin from his lap. "Gentlemen, if you'll excuse me for a moment."

He stood and left the room, leaving Sikes and Nash alone for the first time.

"I apologise."

Sikes' sluggish eyes swivelled to Nash. "What?"

"I apologise for leading them to you, it was never my intent. They used me to get to you, and for that I'm sorry."

The apology was only partially true. He wasn't sorry at all; Sikes was no innocent lamb. But Nash needed an in with the man, and words of contrition seemed the most direct approach.

Waving a floppy hand in his direction, Sikes replied, "Don't sweat it, my dude. That's what these bastards do, they use everyone." He gulped more wine. "Do you remember the last thing you said to me before leaving me for dead in the desert?"

There didn't seem to be any malice in the question. Nash couldn't determine if that was because none was intended, or if it was just masked by the booze.

"It was years ago, I can't..."

"You said to make something of my life. Make it count." Sikes leaned in and peered around for any prying ears. "Well, this wasn't it. I thought it was, at first. I thought I'd been saved and was going to do good for once in my stinking life. I'm sure you've heard the sales pitch by now. Tartarus isn't..." his head swivelled around again; the man was paranoid. Nash didn't know yet if it was justified or not. "... it isn't what you think it is. Well, it is, but it isn't."

"That's suitably vague."

Sikes waved an indiscriminate finger. "You'll find it all out. But back to my point, or indeed *your* point, about making a difference. That was what I was trying to do when I left here."

"By buying a luxury yacht?"

"The yacht was simply the in with those people. A third of Brazil's population live below the poverty line and all of them combined earn just one per cent of the wealth. Not exactly fair and equitable, is it? I was going to help the poor balance things out a bit, like you told me I should. I wanted to make my life count for once. But now here I am, back doing the devil's work."

"What do you mean, the devil's work?"

Opening his mouth to speak, Sikes snapped it shut as soon as Pinchot walked through the door. He poured himself another wine and shrank back into his chair like a sulking teen.

"Problem, Pinchot? Run out of evildoers?"

In reply, Pinchot smiled and gave Nash a chuckle. "Quite the contrary. We've added one to our list."

"Oh, anyone I know?"

"I doubt it, unless you've been hanging out with Venezuelan arms dealers in your retirement?"

"Venezuelan? No."

Pinchot went on to explain that Travis had informed him of an arms dealer who had gone off-script. The CIA had provided him with US currency to supply weapons to the "good rebels" of Venezuela, as in, those who backed American causes. Only trouble was, instead he chose to supply arms to Colombian warlords because they paid better. That was something Pinchot and his organisation couldn't abide. According to him, the CIA had written the arms dealer off their books without even attempting to admonish him for his disloyalty.

In his delivery, Pinchot did his best to radiate a sense of detachment, like he would in an official briefing, but Nash detected an undercurrent of emotion. It appeared he took the betrayal to heart. Was there some connection between Pinchot and the arms dealer, or was he such a patriot he took the betrayal to his country as a personal afront?

"João Rocha is the gentleman's name. He's using the additional funds to start his own drug trafficking side hustle now he's on good terms with the Colombians. He's flooding Guyana with cheap cocaine and heroin, muscling out the opposition with plans to expand to other countries. The cheap heroin has led to twenty reported deaths, but the real number is likely far higher."

Again, Nash was intrigued by how extensive Tartarus's intelligence gathering capabilities were. The way Pinchot spoke, it was as if he had access to all CIA reports on the man. For all Nash knew, he did.

This was no idle chat. As much as Pinchot tried to hide it, he was assessing Nash's reaction to his tale. There was no doubt there was some sort of angle here. Nash knew there would be a test of his loyalty once he joined Tartarus. He sensed it would be coming sooner than he'd thought.

"Rocha is a menace and only growing more so. His organisation is in its infancy with no clear next in line. The whole operation can be stopped before it becomes too big. The CIA and MI6 know what this guy is doing, yet they are doing nothing. We just received intel that he's returned home for the first time in weeks. We need the man eliminated." All cordiality was washed from Pinchot's tone. "And we want you to kill him."

The shift was as abrupt as it was harsh. Pinchot's face was as hard and unyielding as granite, the gameshow cheeriness a distant memory.

"I don't do assassinations." Nash leaned back and folded his hands in front of him. "Not anymore."

Pinchot tilted his head to the side as if this was the response he'd expected. "Let me tell you about the lovely man, shall I? Not only has this delightful poster child for humanity betrayed his CIA employers and killed countless innocents and not so innocents with his drug ring, his personal tastes are, shall we say, less than acceptable to the wider population. He has a penchant for young boys. He abducts them from the streets of the Dominican Republic, enslaves them, rapes them repeatedly and discards them when he's bored or they get too old. And by discard, I mean murder and dump them in a ditch somewhere."

"How do you know all this?" Nash did his best to retain a sense of professional detachment, but realised he'd failed.

"Because when he tried to murder one, he missed."

Pinchot explained that one of Rocha's slaves had been abducted at the age of seven from the poverty-stricken streets of Barrio Malo, which unironically means "bad neighbourhood". A place so impoverished it lacked basic sanitation, had no water or electricity and where violence was a part of life. Forced to do unspeakable acts, the kid was kept chained in a basement with ten others for years. One day Rocha told him he was too old, and he and two other captives were taken to the outskirts of Barrio Malo. The other two died from headshots, but the third boy was only grazed and left for dead in a ditch. He somehow made it out, staggered the streets until strangers helped him find his way to his old neighbourhood. His parents had died years before, and no one knew what had happened to his siblings. Tartarus found him through an application he made to the US consulate. He made a false declaration regarding his parentage while claiming asylum.

"This is who the CIA does business with?"

Pinchot gave an exasperated sigh. "That suit you were wearing on the yacht, can you tell me every piece of cloth was prepared by adults paid a living wage with health care and adequate safety protocols? No, you can't. Here at Tartarus we do a far better job of vetting all our business partners, unlike the CIA. And equally unlike my former employer, here at Tartarus we correct our mistakes. Believe me, you'll be doing the world a favour by taking this human filth out. You'll be saving countless lives."

Nash steepled his fingers. "I see your point, but my answer is still the same. I'm no hitman. It's not what I do."

"Then why did you join us?"

"Last I heard, the word espionage wasn't interchangeable with assassin. I'll investigate for you, I'll use all my years of experience to track your so-called evildoers, but I won't be carrying out wetwork for you. You want that done, find someone else."

Taking his time, Pinchot considered Nash's words. "I suspected this would be your stance. If I'm honest, I was hoping for a different response."

"Well, I wish I still had abs, but we can't have everything."

Sikes held up a tilted glass. "I never had abs." He burped and finished his glass, his eloquent contribution to the conversation apparently at an end.

Drumming his fingers on the table, Pinchot eventually nodded. "I believe we can make this work."

"What happened to the kid?"

"What?" Pinchot blinked at Nash's question.

"The one who escaped Rocha. The kid who tried and failed to get to the US. What happened to him?"

"I... I don't know."

Nash folded his arms. "Seems you're not exactly the magnanimous philanthropic organisation you claim to be."

"Give us time, Nash, give us time." Pinchot leaned forward. "You're in?"

It was plain to everyone at the table—although Sikes may have been too drunk to realise as much—that Nash had only joined Tartarus to save his own life. It was equally plain that Pinchot hoped he would really join them soon. Nash intended to test the hypothesis.

"I want all the evidence for this João Rocha. All of it. Recordings, communications, CIA files, the lot. If he's truly what you say he is, then I'll help you do whatever it is you have to do."

"Short of killing the man?"

"Short of that, yes."

"And if you're satisfied Rocha is indeed the person I describe?"

Nash took the time to refill his glass, leaned back, took a sip and stared Pinchot in the eyes.

"Then I'm in."

FOURTEEN

N ash's binoculars were fogged up. Even in its coldest months, the Dominican Republic's night-time temperature never dipped below twenty degrees centigrade, yet Nash's binoculars were clearly fogged. He put it down to his body temperature being far higher than his surroundings. High up on a jungle hilltop, he was nervous. He was jumpy. More than anything, Nash was angry.

He'd spent days trawling through the mountains of intelligence Tartarus had gathered on Rocha. The evidence was overwhelming. As he'd suspected, Tartarus somehow had access to classified CIA files. There were also Dominican Republic and Colombian National Police reports, Guyana Health Department statistics, eyewitness interviews and Tartarus's own independent surveillance. It all came to the same conclusion: João Rocha had stolen from the CIA to fund a fledgling illicit drug cartel.

That wasn't what made Nash angry.

It had been the vision seen through his binoculars as he observed the house in the valley below. Nash had been on surveillance duty for seven hours. It was now nearly three am, and for the most part he had only the incessant jungle sounds to keep him company.

For the most part.

Nash hit the comms button on the lapel of his tactical vest. "Travis, are you seeing—"

His mostly silent companion on the mission had little to say on the helicopter flight over, at their tactical briefings or when they'd been airlifted into the jungle.

"Yeah, I saw it." The big man was not one for emotion, but Nash detected a hard edge of anger creeping in, even over comms. "We move now."

It wasn't a question.

The two men descended from their perches high above the isolated mansion. They occupied different hills, providing differing views of Rocha's supposed secret hide-out. The multi-storey mansion was an anathema to the lush green rainforest surrounding it, the hulking edifice more suited to the American suburbs.

What Rocha hadn't counted on was the purchase of excess building materials, paid for in cash, arousing the interest of the nearby town's police department. Their report was referred to town planning and then to the Dominican Republic's taxation department, whose interest suddenly dissipated. No doubt bribery had made it disappear from the government's books, but not the CIA's. They knew exactly where to find Rocha's secret hideout, yet they chose to do nothing.

If they had, Nash wouldn't have been subjected to the scene he and Travis had just witnessed.

Through the expansive windows, they had watched a seemingly drugged up Rocha drag a boy by the hair through the lounge into his bedroom. The child couldn't have been more than ten. All the while, Rocha placed his hands on parts of the boy no adult should ever touch on a child. The kid's silent frantic and anguished screams had been obvious even from Nash's great distance.

Rocha's security was minimal. It appeared he assumed his secret base of operations was so remote it would be defence enough. He was wrong. Storming through the jungle towards the illuminated compound, Nash cocked his pistol.

"Two hundred out, slowly making my way forward, over."

Nash acknowledged Travis's message and confirmed he was doing the same. There were only three guards who carried out sporadic patrols. They hadn't been seen for a couple of hours, so it was assumed they'd retired for the night. Sloppy security.

Rocha's guards no doubt knew who they worked for and the kind of man they chose to associate with. And that was exactly the point. They had chosen to work for a man who didn't deserve to be called such, nor to continue to live as one. Rocha was the personification of evil.

That didn't mean Nash wasn't conflicted. As much as he knew deep in his soul the fate Rocha deserved, it still chafed against his vow of non-violence. If there was ever to be an exception to the rule it would be this human filth. He was pleased he had Travis with him so he wouldn't have to make that decision. The operation could easily have been conducted by a single individual, but given Nash's distaste for killing, Travis was present for the final act.

Nash clicked on his comms. "Eyes on guard hut. Lights out, door closed. Over."

"Acknowledged. I'm at the north end, thirty metres away. Over."

Nash was impressed the big man had moved so quickly and stealthily.

Checking his watch, he said, "Thirty seconds. Like we discussed, gut and clean. Over."

"And mark."

The next half a minute passed glacially. Every possible scenario played out in Nash's head. He fell back on his training from years before, focusing on his breathing, visualising his first ten steps, where he would focus his gaze. For the next few minutes he would become a machine, a tool without emotion. And yet, he hoped, a non-lethal one.

The sounds of the jungle at night are unique. Nocturnal animals screech and flitter about, birds flutter and squawk. Huge tropical leaves and branches break away and cascade down a tree, sounding for all the world like an avalanche of adversaries converging on you. Far from relaxing, the jungle at night is a discord of imagined terrors. Nash filtered them all out.

As the final second ticked, he saw Travis move into position. The man was a blur. Nash closed in behind him, covering his back. Travis kicked in the door of the wooden hut, and flashes illuminated its dark interior.

Pistols fitted with a silencer weren't as noiseless as the movies made them out to be. But amid the incessant cacophony of the jungle, the noise barely carried to Nash's position outside the door, let alone to the main house.

In seconds, the only sounds were the raucous jungle. That was, until Travis spoke.

"Nash."

"Hmm?"

"There's only two here."

Instinctively turning towards the hut, Nash pivoted his pistol in the direction of the door, although he never made it that far. In the corner of his eye, he spied a crouching figure with rifle raised. Nash dove.

The shot went overhead as he dive-rolled forward, landing pistol up. With sufficient cover behind a mahogany tree, Nash loosed three shots instinctively.

"Contact, contact, contact."

The shabbily dressed guard didn't dart away to nearby cover; instead he dropped to the ground, seemingly thinking it was the safer option. Nash targeted the dirt in front of his face to educate him otherwise. The minimal body mass of a front-facing, ground-hugging adversary made it difficult for Nash to land non-lethal shots. With sufficient cover behind the tree, Nash was prepared to wait out the guard until he ran out of ammo.

Travis had other ideas.

The ex-CIA agent launched himself sideways from the guard's hut, firing two pistols at once like he was in a John Woo movie. The guard clipped him before he even hit the ground. Nash had no idea if the guard was some savant-level marksman or if he'd fluked the shot, but Travis's upper arm exploded in a burst of red. Bullets flew in all directions.

When Nash next poked his head around the massive tree it was all over. The guard's head was at an odd angle with a hole in the centre of his forehead and a shocked expression on his lifeless face. Travis writhed on the ground, his red-soaked shirt turning the surrounding dirt into bloody mud.

Between clenched teeth, Travis carped, "Motherfucker shot me. Dumb-ass, jungle-living, teeth-missing dumb motherfucker fucking shot me."

"You did leap out at him like you were in a nineties

action flick. For a split second there I thought John Travolta had come to save the day."

Travis flinched when Nash applied pressure to the wound. "I'm Cage, you're Travolta."

Nash stepped into the guard's hut and came back with t-shirts and a belt. As he applied the makeshift tourniquet, he shook his head. "Bullshit. I'm way more Cage than you are. You're totally Travolta."

He tightened the tourniquet to silence any further discussion. Without a word being exchanged, they both understood what Travis's injury meant. He was out of the game.

With the mission incomplete, Nash would need to go it alone. There would be no Travis to make any lethal shots if required. It would all be on him.

Administering the scant medicines in the med kit, Nash left Travis in the guard's hut, doped up and still in pain. As he stood in the doorway, thunder clapped and the rain soon followed. He turned to Travis, unsure if he'd ever see the man again. For all sorts of reasons.

The mansion was virtually empty. Nash stalked through the dark halls, gun up and finger on the trigger, soaked to the skin. The constant thrum of tropical rain and the odd flash of lightning gave the whole place an oddly gothic feel. After sweeping the ground floor to ensure there were no rogue guards, Nash knew where his next port of call would be.

Minutes later he stood, making a puddle at the foot of Rocha's bed. Heavy chains were attached to each of the four bed posts. The cuffs were worn and stretched with use. There were two naked figures laying on the silk sheets: Rocha and the young boy Nash had seen dragged upstairs.

Nash cocked his pistol. In the silence of the room, the action sounded like cannon fire. Both awoke with a start.

Addressing the boy, Nash said, "Anda pequeño. Espera afuera. No quieres ver esto."

Which translated to, "Go, little one. Wait outside. You don't want to see this."

The kid didn't have to be told twice. No matter what your background, a man with a gun is someone you generally take advice from. Nodding profusely, he raced out the room.

Disdain etched on every feature, Nash tossed Rocha a nearby robe. "Ponte la ropa."

Leaving the robe untouched, Rocha placed his hands behind his head and examined Nash from combat boot to grey hair. Pretty ballsy. Literally.

"Who the fuck are you?" he asked in English.

"The cuffs." Nash flicked his gun to the wrist restraints near Rocha. "Put them on."

He waggled his gun to emphasise the point. With an annoyed grumble, Rocha complied. "Who sent you?"

"No one you need to worry about."

"Who said I'm worried?" He clasped his hands together on his naked chest, chains clinking as he did. "Now I guess the question is how much this is going to cost me. What's your price?"

The words flowed from Rocha's cracked lips with so much ease it was clear he was used to buying his way out of trouble. It was also obvious he'd never met Mason Nash.

If there was ever a human being alive who deserved Nash to break his non-murderous vow it was the human virus before him. The man posed no benefit to the human race, bar himself. He wasn't a megalomaniac dictator or some power hungry genocidal general. In some ways, he was much worse. A little man with little power, but what he had, he used to bring only misery, pain and death.

Nash shook his head. "You won't be buying your way out of this one, Rocha."

The statement amused rather than scared him. "You going to kill me, American?"

"For one, I'm deeply offended you think I'm American. Secondly, no, I'm not going to kill you." Nash tucked his pistol into his shoulder holster.

The surprise in Rocha's eyes made them stand out comically. "Then... then what? You're letting me go?"

"I didn't say that, now did I?"

Keeping his eyes trained on the confused arms and drug dealer, Nash opened the bedroom door. One by one, children entered the room, eleven in all, including the one Nash had sent from the room. He was draped in an oversized t-shirt the other boys had sourced from somewhere.

On securing the first floor, Nash's first destination had been the basement, where he'd liberated the captive children. The wretches lived in squalor. Half the basement was behind a cage, where there weren't enough beds for them all. Many slept on the dirt floor. There was no toilet, only a bucket. They were all huddled together for warmth and protection.

The boys were aged from about eight to twelve. These were not wide-eyed happy kids. Each one of them was sullen-eyed, their eyes bearing a hard-edged hatred that would be terrifying in a war veteran, but was heartbreaking in a child. At first Nash tried to convince them to flee, telling them what his mission was.

The children had another idea. In fact, they'd demanded it, so vehemently Nash wondered if they'd go through him to get to it.

On entering the bedroom, each child carried a weapon, be it a pipe, a fire poker, a kitchen knife or a golf club. Every one of them glared at Rocha with undeniable hatred, propagated through years of torture and abuse.

In all his years, Nash had to admit he'd never seen fear like he saw in Rocha's eyes when he finally realised what his fate would be. Struck mute, he gawped open-mouthed at Nash, eyes pleading.

In response, Nash tilted an imaginary hat and left the group to their activity, closing the door on his way out. Thunder clapped in the distance. He'd gone all of three paces before he heard the first scream. He was sure it would not be the last.

When Nash made his way to the guard's hut, Travis was on the outer edge of lucidness. When the injured man saw him, Nash wasn't sure if it was surprise or relief on his face. He'd lost more blood, but the flow had slowed. Some colour had returned to his face.

"It's done?"

"It's done."

With a grunt, Travis picked up his radio transmitter. "Base, two for extraction."

"No."

Travis's head snapped around. "No?"

"No." Nash's eyes locked on Travis. "Thirteen for extraction."

"We're not taking..."

"Then what's it all for? You claim we're the good guys? Then let's do some good. We're in the middle of the damn jungle. Where are those kids going to go? How will they survive? They might have parents, they might not. Even if they do manage to get out, how the hell are they meant to find them alone? We can't leave children here to die."

A crackling voice over the transmitter said, "Say again, over?"

Travis's eyes narrowed. He clicked the transmitter. "Base, I think you're going to have to put the boss on the line."

"What? Why?"

Travis sighed as he glared at Nash. "There's been a change of plan."

CHAPTER
FIFTEEN

"Did you pack your toothbrush?"

"Yes!"

While the volume was annoyed, the tone was anything but. Ramon's ever-present broad grin also gave it away. As he and Nash stood near the helipad of the Tartarus compound in the old fort, a helicopter approached in the distance.

It had taken weeks, but nearly all the boys recovered from Rocha's hellhole had been returned to their astounded families. The parents had given up hope of their children ever returning alive. The few children without families had been placed in expensive foster arrangements. All were provided with mental health services, a lifetime of education and a trust fund to help rebuild their shattered lives.

Nash had held Tartarus to the ethics they were so quick to expound.

The last of the group was Ramon, the poor kid Nash had found in Rocha's bedroom. Once they'd left the mansion and arrived at Tartarus, the two had formed a fast friendship. While they searched for Ramon's parents, Ramon attached himself to his saviour and Nash found he enjoyed the boy's company. The kid possessed incredible resilience, and within days was impressing the staff of the compound with his magic tricks. He and Nash shared every meal for a week, until the news came that his mother and father had been found on the outskirts of Barrio Malo.

The helicopter was to take him home. Nash finally knew where the Tartarus compound was located—the Puerto Rico coast. The hop to the Dominican Republic wasn't excessive. The first flight out of Rocha's lair had the boys enraptured the entire way.

Nash received the fifth farewell hug in as many minutes.

"Do we have time to see the orange car before we go?"

Nash smiled and shook his head. Ramon's bottom lip dropped into a pout.

The highlight of the Tartarus compound was Pinchot's prized Lamborghini, bright orange and gleaming. Nash still had no idea where Pinchot would drive it, but he had an obvious fixation with it. All the boys drooled over the sportscar but Pinchot had refused to let them anywhere near it, let alone sit in it. There seemed to be at least one thing on the planet Pinchot loved.

Returning to the bittersweet farewell, Nash reminded himself Ramon would soon be in the hands of his loving family. That, he would be eternally grateful for.

"Ramon."

"Hmmm?" The boy was fascinated by the sight of the approaching helicopter, unable to tear his eyes away from it.

"I have one last thing for you."

The boy finally turned. "But you have already given me so much, el caballero. I will go to school," he flashed his trademark grin, "and I will be the best student, you'll see! And the money for my family to eat, to rent a house in the city. You have given us so much!" His grin grew wider. "And my toothbrush!"

Nash chuckled. "Yes, and it is no more than you deserve, Ramon. But this," he pulled out a folded piece of paper from his pocket and tucked it into the boy's tiny hand, "is different. This is for me. Please only open it when you get home. Can you promise me that?"

"Of course, señor. Anything you ask is yours."

As the helicopter came in for its final approach, all Nash could do was nod to the boy. The pilot slid open the side door of the Bell UH-1 Iroquois and motioned for Ramon to come over. He'd made the run with groups of the other children and always offered them a ready smile.

Ramon turned to Nash with tears welling up, but doing his best to be brave. Nash gave him one last hug, and it seemed the boy would never let go. When he finally did, he gave Nash a salute and ran towards the waiting Huey. Once strapped in, the helicopter took off. Ramon continued to wave at Nash until the two lost sight of one another.

Once his friend was out of sight, Nash headed towards the Tartarus gym. Located next to the armoury, it was stocked with the latest equipment. Since returning from the Dominican Republic, Nash had turned his attention to getting himself fit and had begun to train. Hard.

Within days he felt his old body coming back; the one he'd had before the indolent history teacher became his persona. Some days he felt like he was in the body he'd had twenty years before. He also reacquainted himself with weapons, new and old. He honed his skills, once again becoming the lethal weapon he'd once been, but this time without the lethal part. Although the paper targets on the firing range took a hammering.

As he trained and sweated, Nash knew the successful mission had put him in the good books with Pinchot and Tartarus. He knew he wasn't fully trusted yet, but felt he was on his way to earning it. Although they still hadn't given him a laptop, phone or access to the outside world. He wondered when that time would come.

Pinchot didn't even seem that mad that Nash had altered the parameters of the mission to save the children, and the extra cost and logistics of sending them home and funding their educations.

Nash was determined to find out more about exactly who and what Tartarus was. He'd been conducting his own investigation and now needed to fill in some blanks. He showered, changed and sought the man who could provide the final answers he needed.

In the last few weeks, Sikes' mood hadn't improved. Nor had his sobriety.

Quickly learning that the best time to talk to the surly American was in the morning, before his first lunchtime tipple, Nash did his best to forge an uneasy friendship. It was easier than he'd expected. Given Sikes' penchant for drinking and general unpleasantness, he'd quickly alienated nearly every member of Tartarus. It was a situation Nash used to his advantage.

The two had taken to walking the perimeter of the old fort before lunch, forming a bond like outsiders the world over. As they stopped at the outermost part of an ancient parapet overlooking a ragged cliff and the churning sea below, Sikes doubled over, gasping for air. Unlike Nash, he wasn't using this time to regain a youthful physique. In fact, he gave the impression he was on a mission to bring on a heart attack or alcohol poisoning.

"Do you like it?" Nash lifted one leg onto the stone wall and stretched his hamstring. "Working for Tartarus, I mean."

Sikes sniffed. "I like taco Tuesday."

Nash had to admit the weekly taco night was a highlight. But that wasn't exactly what he was getting at.

"Taking down Rocha and freeing those kids made me feel pretty good. At least the bastard's funds are going to go somewhere useful. Pinchot claimed he'd managed to hack into Rocha's accounts in the Caymans."

"*He'd* managed to hack in, had he?"

It was the reaction Nash had been hoping for; the exact reason he'd worded it the way he had.

Nash did his best to bob his head as if conceding the point. "They really rely on you for all this, don't they?"

"Pinchot would have shit without me. Tartarus would still be nothing but a bunch of clueless ex-spies sitting around a card table in the middle of Massachusetts with their thumbs up their butts, an idea for a private spy agency and fuck all else."

Massachusetts is an interesting detail, Nash thought.

It was the most lucid Sikes had been in days. Nash intended to press the advantage.

"They obviously wouldn't have all this," Nash waved his arms around the vast compound to emphasise the point, "without your brains. How did you do it? I'm guessing you didn't rig the mega millions lotto." Nash paused. "Did you?"

"No." Sikes peered into the distance wistfully. "Although that's an idea I hadn't thought of. Nah, this little start-up applied my personal algorithms to multiply the bad guys' money. I exploit market economics in all sorts of ways—washing, pump and dump, churning, spoofing. You name it, my little bots are all over it. Currency manipulation is a good one too. You heard how the Yen got smashed a few months ago? That was me." Sikes was warming to the topic, his face brighter than Nash had seen it in weeks. "Oh, those fucken' crypto bros are a godsend. Throw a couple of posts on Reddit and we fund this place for months."

It seemed Sikes was indeed the brains of the autonomous spy agency. Nash wondered exactly who the head of it all was. It wasn't Pinchot, that much was clear.

Although the ex-CIA man big-noted himself, especially in front of Nash, Pinchot had cryptically yielded several big decisions to "beyond the board". That meant there was someone higher than the board, someone at the very top of the pyramid.

Knowing he wouldn't get the answer so soon, Nash decided to ask a different question. "I'm wondering why they decided to set up their headquarters here."

Sikes' laugh came as a surprise. He shook his head. "This isn't Tartarus's headquarters, man. This is a little temporary training facility, nothing more than that."

Nash thought about the extensive fit-out, equipment and dozens of personnel. All the helicopters, chefs and armaments. He'd spent weeks thinking about the funds required for such a vast undertaking, only to learn this was only a small piece of Tartarus. Now he had to wonder how big this operation really was.

Stretching his arms overhead and doing his best to sound laid back, Nash asked, "Just how many people actually work for Tartarus?"

Glancing up, Sikes gave him a sneer. "That's a Pinchot question."

"But he's not here." Nash peered towards the compound in the distance. "I mean, I can yell pretty loud, but not that loud."

Giving a shrug as if to say, *what the hell*, Sikes replied, "Last count, a smidge under two thousand."

Nash had to grab the stone parapet for stability before he toppled over. *Two thousand?* Had he heard that right?

Sikes went on. "That's excluding those we pay a fee to for every piece of intelligence they pass our way. Pinchot's hoping to double the operation by the end of the year, but the board thinks that's too aggressive."

It was far bigger than Nash would have imagined. How had such an organisation been created under the noses of every secret service organisation on the planet? The concept of Tartarus going undetected for so long gave credence to the possibility its own people had infiltrated the very organisations that should have detected it. That line of thinking was one horrifying road Nash wasn't quite prepared to go down. At least, not yet.

Ill-gotten gains multiplied by stock manipulation and no doubt other illegal practices meant Tartarus could conceivably have an endless supply of funds for their operation. The limiting number of Tartarus's staff would be their only threshold. Two thousand could achieve a hell of a lot, but it wasn't quite an all-powerful, all-encompassing secret service operation. At its height during World War Two, the OSS, the precursor to the CIA, employed over twenty thousand employees. Although Tartarus wasn't fighting a war.

At least, Nash didn't think they were.

Not yet, anyway.

Several days later, Nash and Pinchot sat at a table on the balcony overlooking the compound and the coastline beyond. They shared an early supper in what was essentially an extension of Pinchot's office. The balcony was high on a grassy hill, the highest point in the compound. Within arm's length was Pinchot's well-stocked drinking cabinet and humidor of fine cigars. There was a chill in the air, a light frost creeping in. The sun was setting, illuminating the vast ocean in a washed-out orange glow. Hands on the railing, Nash took in the scene.

"You look a million miles away." Pinchot poured Nash a glass of 2016 Pomerol Château Gombaude-Guillot. A particularly excellent drop. "What are you thinking?"

"If you put one lasagne on another lasagne you still only have one lasagne."

Responding with a confused shake of his head, as if to dismiss Nash's frivolity, Pinchot went on. "You've been here for a while now. Is there anything our little operation needs? Some tweaks to make it better than it already is?"

"Like a second sauna, hey boss?"

Pinchot gave a slanted grin. "Boss?"

Chuckling, Nash said, "You've been called worse things."

"I know. Some by you."

Both men shared a chuckle. Both men forced it.

A bell rang and the pair sat down as dinner was served on a pristine white tablecloth. Placing his equally pristine white napkin in his lap, Pinchot raised an eyebrow. "I hear you've been poking around and asking questions about the organisation." Pinchot did his best to sound nonchalant, but failed miserably. He was all chalant.

"Well, in the absence of a corporate polo shirt I thought it wise to find out all I can about this enterprise I've joined."

"I don't know if I'd label extracting information from Sikes as wise, per se." Pinchot poked at his steak. "One might even infer you were investigating us."

And there it is, Nash thought. For weeks Pinchot's affable persona had been exactly that, a façade. This darker, more menacing tone fitted him like an old pair of jeans. Well-worn and comfortable.

"I'm a spy. Finding things out is what I do." Nash hadn't intended to go down this path so soon into the dinner he'd requested, yet here he was.

Pinchot held up a finger. "Ex-spy. A real spy wouldn't need a chaperone on a mission, because a real spy will kill when it is required."

"I wonder why killing is so important to you? Shouldn't we be upholding a superior set of morals? Aren't we supposedly the good guys?"

Pinchot raised an eyebrow. "Supposedly? Are you calling João Rocha an innocent now, are you?" He put down his cutlery. "You can't tell me the world isn't a better place without that filth in it."

Nash gave a frown of agreeance. The world was indeed a better place without the likes of Rocha. But Nash had other reasons to question Tartarus's methods and unrestrained dominion.

"I don't have a problem with taking out murderous arms and drug dealers who rape little boys..."

"I'm so glad to hear it."

"But I want to know who watches the watchers. What if the next one isn't as clear cut as Rocha? At least with a government-run secret service you have government oversight, the National Security Act, a Director of National Intelligence, the cabinet, the President—"

"Bureaucracy, red tape, political agendas." Pinchot

threw down his napkin. "I thought we'd been through this? We're not some Cold War evil empire relic. We're here to serve the world. Our aim is to take down the Rochas who have plagued humanity for far too long because of a lack of political will or because bribery, legal or otherwise, ensures so-called intelligence agencies look the other way. We're going to shape the world, Nash. I want you to be a part of it. Tartarus will use its powers to bring down those who enjoy the exploitation of others. Slave traders. Terrorists. The CIA and MI6 know who these bastards are but do nothing. We're going to take them all down."

"And if anyone stands in your way?"

"They'll be dealt with."

"Suitably menacing and vague. I wonder what that means exactly?"

Pinchot groaned. "What is this really about, Nash? You joined us for a reason."

"One man's 'joined' is another man's 'shanghaied'."

Slamming his fists on the table, Pinchot's face grew red. "We're the good guys here!"

Calmly, Nash replied, "Even the Nazis thought they were the good guys."

"Fuck you."

"Touché."

Inhaling unevenly, Pinchot clenched and unclenched his fists. "We're going to do what no spy agency has ever done. We're able to operate unrestrained, take down those who need to be eliminated. We'll use the most sophisticated intelligence gathering network ever created to influence world leaders into doing what's right."

"Sounds like you're manipulating the world, not serving it."

In the distance there was a series of flashes and pops.

Pinchot gave the distant sky scant regard. "Locals and their fireworks. I wonder what this celebration is for." He shook his head, refocusing his attention. "What we're doing will shape the twenty-first century and beyond. We have tentacles everywhere. Every major intelligence community has been compromised. Tartarus will soon be the world-shaping order no government secret-service organisation could ever dream of being. Whether you choose to believe it or not, Nash, we *are* the good guys."

"Operation Sanskrit."

Pinchot visibly gulped. "That was a mistake, yes."

"Operation Landmark."

A false smile couldn't hide Pinchot's eye twitch. "You're well informed."

"Operation Cantata."

Pinchot folded his arms. "Where did you find out about that?"

Nash took a long sip of his wine. "You should really put better locks on your server room doors."

Operation Sanskrit was a Tartarus mission from three months before. It was a clusterfuck from the outset. Originally designed as an operation to take down the financier of several Middle Eastern terrorist organisations, it was based on out-of-date information and sketchy third-hand intel that smacked of score settling. Instead of taking down the single objective, Tartarus missed him entirely and instead murdered a gang rival's family. The victims included seven children, three grandparents and three wives who were guilty of nothing more than being related to the enemy of the snitch who provided the address.

That was nothing compared to Operation Landmark. Operatives were tasked with taking out the stronghold of Somali pirates terrorising the Gulf of Aden. Instead of destroying the headquarters, Tartarus eliminated the entire fishing village called Qosoltire, where the headquarters was located. One hundred and thirty men, women and children were burned alive after Tartarus set off a thermobaric weapon, also called a fuel-air bomb. It created a fireball three hundred metres tall. There was nothing left of the victims to bury.

Operation Cantata was perhaps the worst of them all. The target wasn't a terrorist. The target wasn't pirates. The target wasn't a drug dealer, a slave trader or an illegal arms dealer. No, the CIA data analyst was guilty of nothing more than being good at her job. Having only been at Langley for seven months, Trisha Adams had followed a data trail leading to Tartarus's door. That, they couldn't stand. Garrotted in her bed, the local news agencies reported a serial killer was on the loose. Little did they know it was far worse.

This had been the mission that broke Sikes and forced him to flee. He was the one who'd identified Trisha and sent assassins to murder her in her bed. His rose-coloured glasses came off that day. Two days later, he escaped.

Nash and Pinchot glared at one another across the table. Nash half suspected Pinchot would simply shoot him on the spot. When the bullet didn't come, he stood and opened Pinchot's prized humidor. Nash checked his watch. It was a few seconds before six.

Picking up Pinchot's lighter without asking, Nash lit a Cuban. "You asked me before if there was anything this operation needed."

Grinding his teeth, Pinchot growled, "So what do you think we need, Nash?"

"A stock management system."

Pinchot jerked backwards in surprise. "What?" He hadn't expected that reply. "Why would we need that?"

Nash took a puff and placed his hands behind his head. "Nobody seems to have noticed I've been taking vast amounts of explosives from the armoury over the past few days."

"Why would you—" Colour drained from Pinchot's face. "Define vast amounts..."

The first explosion lit up the sky. Nash had made sure his first timed explosive charge was the armoury itself. The C4 did its job, and then some. The explosion obliterated the semi-buried bunker, as well as the nearby gym and part of the barracks. The second took out the electricity substation. The third and fourth destroyed the north and south gates. The final one blew up Pinchot's prized Lamborghini. It had no strategic value, Nash just wanted to see Pinchot's face when it exploded.

He wasn't disappointed.

Reeling from the carnage unfolding below, Pinchot's enraged face spat venom. "I'll fucking kill you!"

Diving for his jacket, Pinchot lunged for an object he'd never find. As his hand delved into his pocket, his face told Nash he hadn't found what he sought. Mainly because it was in Nash's hand.

Aiming the Browning at Pinchot, Nash motioned for him to sit back down. "You should watch the next bit. It will be fascinating."

To the north, a dozen well-armed black-clad fighters stormed through the smoking ruins of the gate. The team made short work of the disorientated Tartarus security guards. The first through the breach had long raven hair tied back in a ponytail. Even though he couldn't see her tattoos,

Nash immediately realised who led the assault. Eva Destruc-tion lived up to her name and charged headlong into the compound, firing a semi-automatic with uncanny accuracy.

Watching Pinchot's face, Nash knew he had seen her too. Utter confusion dripped from his features.

Nash puffed on the cigar. "Stock management is very important."

CHAPTER
SIXTEEN

It all started in São Paulo.

In Nash's formidable experience, planning for contingencies was never a wasted activity. Knowing that boarding Sikes' megayacht would leave them exposed and cornered, Eva had organised a Royal Navy backup. The newly launched *HMS Immortalité* was based on the US Navy's Zumwalt-class destroyer and boasted a radar cross-section more akin to a fishing boat than a warship. Perfect for shadowing a yacht that had no idea it was being followed.

But following was one thing. Nash had no idea Eva had survived the leap into the churning ocean until the instant he saw her breach the gate. She'd had to have survived long enough for the Royal Navy vessel to pick her up. The tracking beacon in her bracelet would have helped them zone in, but there was always a strong possibility that Eva had died in the ocean. From his vantage point on the balcony, Nash was beyond overjoyed to see her not only in the flesh, but leading the charge into the compound.

Ramon had kept his promise. The note Nash had passed

him several days before had been the spark to light the fuse. It was a detailed description on how to get a note to Paul Cavendish at MI6 via the British Embassy. The message contained all Nash knew about Tartarus, including the missions where civilians had died at their hands. It also detailed when and how to launch the attack, as well as detailed diagrams of the compound, its defences and security.

The fireworks at sunset were to let Nash know everything was in place.

A scream of rage beside Nash reminded him he wasn't alone.

Pinchot's red face glowed with wrath. "Do you know what you've done?"

"Missed out on dessert?"

"You've ruined years of work. Thousands could have been saved. We were helping the world."

Nash let out a sigh. The cold night air turned it to vapour dancing in the air. "No, you weren't, Pinchot. What you *were* doing was killing innocents. *Innocent* families, *innocent* fishing villages, *innocent* office staff. Why? Because you have some twisted delusion that you're the good guys. You're not. Good guys don't murder data analysts because they're efficient at their job. They don't burn fishing villages full of the elderly. You were so caught up in your own delusions of grandeur you forgot the reality of what you were *actually* doing. Civilians died. And they'd continue to if you were allowed to keep doing what you've been doing. Sure, oversight can be limiting, but it's there for a reason. An unrestrained, uncontrolled secret service isn't what the world needs."

"Is this where you tell me the world needs less violence? If so, you'll need to get me a bucket first."

"No." Nash raised his pistol. "The world needs less you."

He lifted the gun; his finger caressed the trigger. It would be easy. All he needed was for his motor cortex to send a message through the spinal cord, down his arm to the muscles controlling his finger. It would take a fraction of a second. He'd done it thousands of times. It was like breathing.

Even more than he had with Rocha, Nash felt compelled to fire. Yes, Rocha was a vile, evil smear of a human being, but the man at Nash's feet was perhaps far worse. Overloaded with power, resources and knowhow, Pinchot could shape the world, and not for the better. The jury was still out as to whether he truly believed he was the benevolent force he claimed to be. Regardless, his track record suggested his destructive path would only grow as his power did. It was time to bring the whole enterprise to an end before the world paid the price.

As if sensing Nash's internal turmoil, Pinchot ratcheted down his anger, at least momentarily.

"We both know you're not going to kill me."

"I'm not entirely sure *we* do." The pistol felt heavy in Nash's hand.

In the distance, the sound of the battle had intensified. Nash assumed Tartarus forces had rallied and were mounting a counterattack.

Face hardening once more, Pinchot flashed his fangs. "I wanted to kill you the moment you arrived here!"

Nash tilted his head. "Then why didn't you?"

"You tortured me for hours. I'll return the favour tenfold!"

Before Nash could respond, the door to the office was yanked open and Travis bounded in, Uzi submachinegun in hand. Indeed, it was one hand. His left arm was in a sling following the injury he'd sustained in the Dominican Republic. It took Travis all of a second to assess the situation; his boss on the ground and Nash with a gun in his face. As the battle raged below, Travis twisted the submachinegun towards the man who had saved his life in the jungle only weeks before.

With the gun trained on Pinchot, Nash was at a disadvantage. The big man had the drop on him, even though he was one-handed. Nash was cornered and outgunned, and Travis's face made it clear he wasn't particularly pleased Nash had a gun trained on his boss.

Nash did the only thing he could think of. He smiled. "Are we still good for 'Islands in the Stream' at karaoke night?"

In reply, Travis flicked off the safety and tightened his grip on the Uzi.

All three men clenched their jaws, each silently waiting for another to make a move. Every muscle tense, every sense heightened. With a groan, Nash resigned himself to his next move.

Feinting left, he dove right, pivoting the Browning towards Travis. Firing, he forced the big man to dive for cover, which he did, landing awkwardly and no doubt hurting his damaged arm. Nash knew it was only a temporary reprieve.

Travis had all the advantages. More cover, more firepower, more everything. For Nash, there was only one course of action.

He did the only thing he could. He leapt over balcony.

As he was in mid-air, he called over his shoulder, "And I was going to sing the Dolly parts!"

The reply came in the form of a hail of bullets.

Nash landed with a thud on the grassy hill and let out

an *oof*, the dew of the evening lubricating his rapid descent. He pivoted so his feet faced the balcony and he hurtled headfirst down the steep hill. He wasn't out of trouble. Not by a long stretch.

Travis reached the edge of the balcony, his submachinegun tracing Nash's descent as he steadied his aim. The Uzi wasn't a long-range weapon and Travis's injury meant his aim wouldn't be the greatest, but Nash wasn't about to make it easy for him. He fired precisely and with malice. Unless, that was, you were a wooden railing. On either side of Travis, Nash embedded bullets in the railing, forcing him to flinch and re-aim, and spoiling successive shots. Nash was relentless, all the while sliding further and further away from the balcony. Every time Travis attempted to target him, Nash fired. Again and again. As he expended the last bullet from the Browning, he saw Travis retreat in disgust and aggravation.

Amid the chaos Nash allowed himself a small measure of pride at his daring escape. Tossing aside his empty weapon, the hill levelled out and he skidded to a stop.

Five machine guns hovered over his face.

Nash gulped and put up his hands. He didn't have much choice in the matter. It was dark and he couldn't clearly see the gun owners, but what he saw was enough to keep him on the soggy ground, remaining immobile until he was advised to do otherwise.

"Dude, you know how hard it is to get grass stains out?"

Nash knew that voice. He missed that voice.

The owner of said voice made a sharp motion with her hand and all machine guns transformed from combative to protective. The small team scanned for further targets. Nash only had one.

He scrambled to his feet and threw his arms around Eva Destruction. "I'm glad you didn't drown."

"Me too." Eva hugged him hard, took a step back and beamed. "Although I'm pretty sure I swallowed half the Southern Atlantic."

"You've swallowed worse."

Eva punched his arm. "You finally get me."

Eva quickly brought him up to speed. The team she was with was part of a combined CIA and MI6 operation. With evidence tying Tartarus to the bombing of Qosoltire and the murder of Trisha Adams, neither organisation could sit it out any longer. The murder of an MI6 agent without due process had no doubt compelled his ex-employer into action. Whoever had infiltrated both organisations could not hold back the avalanche of senior leadership mandating action. Eva made sure she was, in her words, part of the party.

"And Nnadi?" Nash asked.

"Total double agent." Eva shook her head in disgust. "We went over her entire career with a fine-tooth comb and discovered so much shady shit."

Pinchot hadn't lied about Nnadi, at least. Nash still didn't feel bad for blowing up his Lamborghini, though. The thought still made him smile.

"There are three targets." Nash motioned to Eva's sidearm.

She unclipped it and handed him the Glock.

He went on. "Sikes, Pinchot and Travis, Pinchot's 2IC."

Eva nodded in acknowledgement. "I don't know the last one. Is that his first or last...?"

Nash held up his hand and shook his head. "My guess is they'll be heading north. That's where the nearest town is and the highway out of here. South offers no cover and leads only to high cliffs. If we can—"

Nash was cut off by an explosion to their right. An orange fireball illuminated the night.

Shielding her eyes, Eva said, "That wasn't us."

"I know. It was the server room. They're going scorched earth."

From the direction of the server room a figure sprinted awkwardly, his arm in a sling.

Nash pointed in his direction. "That would be Travis."

As one, the six of them sprinted. With the darkness of the night now complete, the spot fires the only illumination, the scene was a series of shadows, flashes and flickering images lit only by the various blazes engulfing the compound.

Nash was the first to get within firing range. The big man was running parallel and slightly ahead of them, heading towards the motor pool, his plastered arm now free from its sling. He carried an Uzi in one hand and didn't appear to have spotted them. Nash halted, raised the Glock and fired once. Travis went down.

One of Eva's compatriots slowed beside Nash and tutted. "Why the leg?"

"Because you can't interrogate a—"

On the ground, Travis twisted and raised his weapon. His plastered arm slowed his lumbering movement, and even in the flickering half-light, his anger and fear were unmistakeable.

"Don't!"

Nash's plea fell on deaf ears.

Travis strafed his fire in a wide, undisciplined arc. It was a futile effort. The Uzi's range was limited and he was up against more and better armed opponents. Before Nash could utter another word of protest, Eva's team pummelled Travis with countless bullets, turning the big proud man into nothing more than pulverised meat.

It was a senseless waste. The man had saved Nash's life, and he his, and now it was all for nothing. Nash had to turn away.

Inhaling deeply, he forced himself to remain on mission. This wasn't over. Not by a long stretch. He turned to Eva.

"If he was headed towards the motor pool..."

Without finishing the thought, he broke into a run. The others followed.

In the distance, beyond a small stone wall, the motor pool was mostly a charred ruin, thanks to Nash's petty vengeful bomb. Near the remnants of the north gate, the pool offered the best chance of escape, no matter what side you were on.

It just so happened, the bad guys got there first.

Amid the smouldering ruins of vehicles, he saw two figures. They must have picked through the remains and found the only two functional vehicles left within the confines of the chain link fence. Two motorbikes. The two men wheeled them towards the motor pool gate. Sikes and Pinchot were about to make a break for it.

Not if Nash had anything to do with it.

Issuing orders to the group, who definitely didn't report to him, Nash intended to surround the two before they managed to start the motorbikes. Unfortunately, there were others who had a different agenda.

Eva saw them before Nash did. She grabbed him by the neck and shoved him to the ground, screaming, "Everyone down!"

Three Tartarus guards opened fire as Eva's team kissed

the grass behind the small stone wall. Pinchot's men were situated at the far end of the motor pool, positioned to cover their boss's escape. The small group's tactics were well honed. One fired while one covered and the third reloaded. It was an effective strategy. Inconvenient, but effective.

"Okay, you two on the right lay down suppressing fire. You two to the left make a feint to the left, allowing Eva and myself to make it to that ridge over there. Then on a designated signal we focus our fire on…"

Nash stopped when Eva made a gesture. It entailed her fist travelling in an up and down jerking motion. He raised a challenging eyebrow.

"Cool strategy, dude. I mean, well thought out and all. But I have a slightly different approach, if you don't mind?"

Pulling a hand grenade from her flak jacket, a wicked grin crossed Eva's ruby lips. Nash had no choice but to return the grin and tilt his head in acquiescence.

Eva pulled the pin and threw the grenade in a perfect arc to land between the three combatants. The explosion sent all three to the ground in agony. Soon all but one stopped their wailing. The injured man was bloodied up the left side of his body, his arm lying limply by his side. In defiance of his injury and the deaths of his comrades, he lifted his machine gun and returned fire.

Nash shook his head. "Why is he still fighting for men who are escaping without them?"

"They're fanatics." Eva poked her head over the stone wall for a second before ducking low again. "This thing is like a cult now. Logic left the chat long ago."

Eyeing the gate of the motor pool, Nash realised they weren't going to get there in time. Pinchot had already kick-started his Diesel motorcycle and was gesturing to Sikes, showing him how to start his. With a growl, Nash leaned over to one of Eva's men and snatched his Ruger long-range rifle.

He didn't trust Eva's team to avoid delivering a lethal blow, so Nash decided to take the shot himself. Lining up the scope, Nash exhaled, ignoring the complaints of the rifle's owner. He took aim at the closest bike. His finger twitched, and a fraction of a second later the Diesel's rear tyre blew out.

Pinchot's remaining man returned fire. Through gaps in the stone fence, Nash saw an exchange by the gate. He couldn't hear it, but it was plain as a politician's Spotify playlist what they were discussing. Sikes pointed at Pinchot's bike as if to say, there's enough room for two. Pinchot said something as he shook his head. Sikes more vehemently pointed to the rear of the bike and threw his hands wide, likely saying, "come on".

Pinchot's answer came swiftly.

Sikes' head snapped back as the bullet hit the dead centre of his forehead. His body collapsed heavily to the ground. A maniacally wide-eyed Pinchot grinned towards where Nash was behind the stone fence. It was obvious what the expression meant. If he couldn't have Sikes' genius, no one could. Sikes would only have slowed Pinchot's escape down, and the man held too many secrets to be left alive.

Pinchot dropped the Diesel into gear and flicked his wrist on the throttle. Fishtailing out of the motor pool, Pinchot wisely zigzagged, making Nash's next three bullets ineffective as they embedded themselves in asphalt. Within seconds, Pinchot sped out the gate.

With the third and last of Pinchot's men finally

succumbing to his injury, Eva's team raced towards the now-vacant pool.

"Find anything that still moves!"

Eva's team did precisely that, rummaging through wrecked vehicles. They stepped over Sikes. There was no doubt the man was dead. His once-brilliant mind had been blown out the back of his skull.

The oldest of the team threw still-smouldering debris to the side. "There's another bike here, it looks okay, it's under this..." He picked up a chunk of charred plastic with a badge on the hood. "Why would anyone blow up a Lamborghini?"

Nash ignored the question, took hold of the bike and kickstarted it.

Eva yelled, "How are you going to take him out if you can't kill him?"

"I don't know." Nash tucked the pistol into the back of his pants. "I'm making this up as I go along."

Twisting the throttle, Nash spun the back wheel and shot towards the gate. Eva yelled some sort of protest but Nash couldn't hear her. He couldn't hear anything. All he heard were the screams of vengeance in his ears.

CHAPTER
SEVENTEEN

The unilluminated Puerto Rico coastal road flew past. Nash travelled at, quite frankly, a ludicrous speed given the road had no street lights and towns were few and far between. But he never once eased his grip on the throttle. He couldn't. Not now.

If Nash were Pinchot, he'd want to put as much distance between the combined forces of the CIA and MI6 as possible. It was simple maths. The greater the distance, the greater the search area. Pinchot would be in pure survival mode. He had a head start on Nash, but not large enough for him to feel comfortable. Nash had no intention of letting Pinchot feel comfortable. Ever again.

Within minutes Nash reached the nearest town, called Stella. The sleepy little seaside village had a smattering of lights eking its way through open windows. Nash didn't slow down the Diesel, even though he hadn't turned on the headlight. He didn't want Pinchot to know he had a pursuer until it was too late. Ducking low, Nash watched for stray dogs or children crossing the road and gunned the motorcycle to close the gap between him and potentially one of the most dangerous men on the planet.

The ex-CIA man's real intent was unclear, but it was plain by the smattering of intelligence Nash had uncovered that Tartarus was not the benevolent saviour Pinchot had tried to sell it as. In their short time, they had killed so many innocent lives. It didn't matter if their intent was truly benign, their history proved their actions were the opposite. It would only get worse from here. Tartarus had to be silenced before it became too big to bring down. *It might already be too late.*

As Nash sped out of town, a wooden sign advised that the next town was twenty kilometres away. For a fleeting second Nash found it odd that Puerto Rico was an unincorporated territory of the United States yet still used the metric system. His wayward thought was soon cut short when the sign splintered into shards.

Nash turned sharply to see a motorcycle bearing down on him.

Fuck.

He'd been so preoccupied with chasing Pinchot, he hadn't thought the same idea may have occurred to his opponent. Pinchot must have laid in wait in the last town, letting Nash speed though and then taking off after him. Now the hunter had become the prey.

He didn't know these dark, winding coastal roads. He had Pinchot on his tail, firing wildly. Nash was at a severe disadvantage. No backup. No way to communicate to the team back at the compound. He was isolated, disoriented and alone. There was only one thing for it.

Nash gunned it.

Doing his best to channel Steve McQueen in *On Any Sunday*, Nash leant low over the front fork to reduce the drag coefficient. The Diesel wasn't exactly a sports bike, but it had some grunt where it counted. It was unfortunate Nash's opponent had the exact same model, and therefore speed. He'd have to squeeze every last rev out of it.

Using only moonlight to navigate, Nash almost missed a turn in the road and hit dirt. Losing precious seconds to slow and correct his course, he cursed his mistake. Gunning it once more, he sped off at full throttle.

The bike wobbled as a bullet hit it somewhere on its rear fender, but as it kept moving forward he assumed it wasn't a fatal blow. Nash leant even lower and tried to turn the throttle more, even though it was already fully extended. He had to change up the game and he had to do it soon. Maintaining the status quo was only going to give Pinchot all the advantage, and he'd be dead within minutes, likely sooner.

It was plain Pinchot wasn't as familiar with riding as Nash was. He was fine on straight stretches, but lost ground on turns. Nash racked his brains for a way he could turn that to his advantage.

Then he saw it.

In the far distance, streetlights illuminated a tall white pillar in the centre of an empty four-way intersection. As the huge monolith was in the dead centre of the intersection, Nash assumed it was a monument to traffic hazards. Nash didn't care what it commemorated, only that he could use it.

He raced towards it, only decelerating at the last possible moment. Hitting the rear brake to slow, Nash turned the throttle to drive out towards the left, feeding the clutch abruptly as he did. The sharp delivery of power forced the rear wheel to spin and he let the bike slide, keeping the wheel locked all the way until he was virtually at a stop when he abruptly delivered all the power with the clutch. The result was a power slide around the monument and he was headed back the way he'd come, gun in hand, firing at the fast approaching Pinchot.

Neither man slowed, neither stopped firing. They roared towards one another at an absurd speed in a modern and murderous version of jousting.

Nash wasn't entirely sure how it happened. It all transpired so fast.

First, Pinchot's bike erupted in a ball of flames. Nash must have hit the fuel tank. There wasn't even a fraction of a second to celebrate before Nash's front tyre blew out. The wheel wobbled and threw him over the front forks, and suddenly he was sailing through the air.

Landing on the gravel shoulder of the road, he tumbled over and over, seeing nothing but grass and the cold, star-filled night sky. He tumbled and tumbled and tumbled. Then everything went black.

～

"You should be dead, Señor."

An unshaven grey-haired man in overalls spoke in heavily accented English. He seemed half pitying, half in awe as he gawped down at Nash.

Tentatively, Nash moved his limbs. Unbelievably, his arms and legs were intact and still attached. His chest hurt when he inhaled. He'd probably cracked a rib or two, but he could still move relatively well. He motioned for the man to help him sit up. It was painful, but nowhere near as bad as he'd feared when he'd been sailing through the air.

Once he regained his breath, Nash asked, "Where's the other one?"

"The other what, Señor?"

"The other man. There was another man in the accident."

"There is no one."

Nash scanned the road. A beat-up seventies Ford pickup held eight dishevelled men in overalls on the flatbed of the truck, likely on their way home after field work. Nash turned to the old man.

"Thank you for stopping. There is another man somewhere. There were two of us in the accident. He's a wanted man. You need to be careful."

The old man grinned a toothless grin and extracted a machete from behind his back. Where he kept it, Nash had no idea.

"I am always careful, Señor."

The old man let out a fierce whistle and advised those in the truck to fan out and search for a dangerous "gringa". They were all as well armed as the old timer.

After half an hour of searching, they had found nothing besides the burnt-out remains of Pinchot's bike, as well as Nash's crashed Diesel. No charred body. No corpse. No body at all.

It was plain the workers wanted to get home after a hard day's toil. It was equally plain Pinchot was nowhere nearby. He'd somehow vanished.

Pushing his newfound friendship to the limit, Nash asked the truck driver to give him a lift back to the compound. He agreed, but only after dropping the locals home first. Nash thought it a fair trade. It was a long way back to the compound on foot.

When he eventually made it back, battered and bruised, the fighting was at an end. Giving the truck driver a wave of thanks at the north gate, Nash set out to find Eva.

Her taskforce was in clean-up mode. They seemed to be scouring for any Tartarus evidence they could find, as well as covering up any suggestion of their raid. It didn't take long for him to find her; she was at the centre of it all, issuing orders.

When she cast eyes on him she let out a low whistle. "You look like you've been in a gorilla threesome."

"I... I don't know what that means."

"Pinchot?"

"Got away."

"We'll alert local authorities to keep an eye on the air and sea ports, but..."

Eva's voice trailing off told Nash she understood the futility of the effort. Pinchot had worked as an operative in the CIA for years, embedded in the most brutal and unforgiving situations. The man wasn't likely to be picked up by a customs official. No doubt he had a contingency stashed somewhere in country. The man was now a ghost, a vapour. If he didn't want to be found, he wouldn't be.

Surveying the destroyed old fortress, she said, "At least we took down Tartarus."

Shaking his head, Nash sighed, which only hurt his ribs. "I'm afraid not. When I sent the message to Paul I thought this was the extent of Tartarus."

"It's not?"

"No, think of this as their base camp."

She planted her fists on her hips. "As in, there's an Everest?"

Nash's response came in the form of a frown. "This whole thing is apparently much larger than anyone suspected."

"How large?"

"Sikes alleged over two thousand and growing. They

have agents embedded in every major intelligence agency on the planet."

"How is that even possible?"

Without waiting for an answer, Eva let out a surprisingly loud whistle. A nearby medic trotted over, and Eva asked her to give Nash a once over.

While the medic did her thing, Nash chastised himself for the fiftieth time. He'd let Pinchot slip away. He could have been used to find out more about this mysterious and powerful organisation. He wasn't the head of Tartarus. Even the exalted board wasn't the head. There was a force beyond, pulling the strings.

The medic administered plasters and tuts and patched Nash up as best as she could, recommending an X-ray at his earliest convenience to see if he had cracked ribs. Nash thanked her and dry-swallowed the painkillers she'd poured into his hand.

After she left, Nash and Eva stood for some time, taking in the scene.

She sucked in the cold night air. "Now this is all done I assume you'll be wanting to head back to your quiet little country town?"

Nash took his time before he gave a slow shake of his head. "Not yet. There's one little thing I have to do first."

"What's that?"

"I have a rogue covert spy agency to take down."

Eva gave him a curious slant of her lips. "Didn't you just say they're far bigger than anyone could have imagined? We don't know—"

"Who's working for them and who isn't." Nash nodded. "They have people in the best spy agencies in the world. That's how they have access to intelligence from the CIA,

MI6, Mossad, everywhere. That means every spy agency is now our enemy as well."

"Our?" Eva smirked. "You're assuming I'm in this too?"

Nash returned the smirk. "It was an assumption on my behalf, yes."

Eva punched him in the arm. "Like you could keep me away."

He winced. She'd picked a newly formed bruise.

Suddenly Nash felt the weight of the recent events and the monumental task ahead of them. In that instant, he felt every one of his fifty-five years. His body felt heavy and old. He rubbed his grey beard and let out a sigh.

Tartarus would not let this first battle go unavenged. Now they knew they were being hunted, they would stop at nothing to keep their growing organisation safe. Nash realised he and Eva were alone, and up against the best in the world.

As the thrum of a distant helicopter drew closer, Nash gazed out towards the horizon. He realised something. Despite all the physical pain his body felt, all the encroaching dread that enveloped him, for the first time in years, Nash felt truly alive.

The End

To be the first to find out when new novels arrive and to win prizes and get free stuff (who doesn't like free stuff?), sign up for my VIP Book Club at:
https://davesinclair.com.au/newsletter/

ACKNOWLEDGMENTS

This is the eleventh book in what I've only just started calling Eva-verse and you know what? I'm still loving this world, loving these characters. Having said that, it's always scary to start a new series. Luckily I had a great companion along the way. Mason Nash is a blast to write – mainly because I do love a challenge. When I started this book there was a very loud voice in my head yelling HOW DO YOU WRITE ACTION WHEN THE MAIN CHARACTER AVOIDS ACTION??!! I soon discovered it was easier than I thought. There's more in store for our new friend Nash with some turns you won't see coming.

And now - the acknowledgements.

What more can I say about my beautiful and amazing wife? She's my inspiration every day. It's no word of a lie that the Eva-verse wouldn't exist if not for her daily encouragement and support. She's amazing.

To my incredible girls, Quinn and Esther, a huge thank you. They're always encouraging and love to share my bookish wins, although they do think their dad is more famous than I really am even though I keep trying to tell them otherwise!

Every writer needs a tribe and I have an awesome one. Thanks to the G-Mob who are brilliant writers and even better friends. To Craig, Justin, Luke, Nathan, Steve, Kat, Amanda and Amanda, thank you for your support, encouragement and laughs.

A big thank you to my editor Vanessa Lanaway for her tireless work. I love the fact she gets excited with every new book and enjoys the read while she's making it better with each red mark (and there's a lot!).

Thanks to The Cover Collection who did a fantastic job on the covers for the whole series. I love the vibe and how they all come together so well.

There's a sneaky reference in the novel of Gareth Lowndes. He won a competition in my VIP Book Club (which you can join on my website – hint hint) to be murdered horribly. Congrats (?!?) again Gareth!

And to my fabulous Book Ninjas who receive an advance copy of my novels – thank you for the amazing feedback! You guys are brilliant.

Don't be afraid to reach out on Facebook, Twitter, Instagram, Threads, carrier pigeon. It's always great to hear from readers. You can stalk me at all these semi-reputable places:

www.davesinclair.com.au

https://facebook.com/DaveSinclairAuthor/

https://www.instagram.com/davesinclairauthor/

https://twitter.com/thedavesinclair

https://www.goodreads.com/author/show/22167525.Dave_Sinclair

https://www.bookbub.com/authors/dave-sinclair

If you can, please drop a review, it is greatly appreciated. It helps new people discover my work.

Thank you and here's to many more adventures!

Dave

www.ingramcontent.com/pod-product-compliance
Lightning Source LLC
Chambersburg PA
CBHW030628120726
47904CB00006B/2073

* 9 7 8 0 6 4 5 4 1 7 6 7 8 *